GHOST TOWNIES 🐈 BOOK TWO

GHOSTLIGHTED

E.J. RUSSELL

Ghostlighted
Copyright © 2025 by E.J. Russell

Cover design: L.C. Chase, http://lcchase.com
Cover model: Nicholas Katen, photographed by Sam San Román
Edited by Meg DesCamp

ISBN: 978-1-965284-04-9

First edition
July 2025

Contact information:
ejr@ejrussell.com

GHOST TOWNIES ❦ BOOK TWO

GHOSTLIGHTED

E.J. RUSSELL

Foreword

Hello, wonderful reader!

I'm so happy you're here, but I want to give you a little heads-up.

The books in the Ghost Townies series are intended to be read in order, since Maz's knowledge and experience (as well as the challenges that smack him in the face) compound over time. In other words, if you haven't read *Ghostridden*, you'll encounter significant spoilers ahead—and the first chapter might be downright, well, *mystifying* if you're not familiar with the Ghost story world.

If it's been a while since you've read book one (or if you're a risk-taker who likes to plunge right into the middle of things), please be sure to check out the next page for a Ghost Townies refresher/introduction.

Cheers!

—E

GHOST TOWNIES

<u>Folks living (or not) in Ghost, Oregon, as of the end of</u>
<u>*Ghostridden*</u>

Maz Amani - Ghostwriter. Unexpectedly inherited a house in Ghost, Oregon, from his mother's second cousin once removed. In addition to ghostwriting gigs, currently employed organizing the Richdale family archives at Richdale Manor.

Gilgamesh (Gil) - Maz's ginger cat

Oren Buckley - Architect; deceased. Maz's mother's second cousin once removed; named Maz his sole beneficiary in his will.

Avi Felder - Thriller author under the pen name Jake Fields; deceased(ish). Oren's boyfriend, and with Oren, co owner of the house Maz inherited. Died ten years ago at the age of thirty. Still (un)living in the house along with Maz, the only person who can see and speak with him.

Enrique (Ricky) Vargas - Maz's romantic interest whose day job is... still unknown. Godson and nephew of Maz's neighbor, he maintained Maz's house for the ten years between Avi's and Oren's deaths at no charge.

Taryn Pasternak-McHale - Attorney. Ghost native and now Maz's BFF.

Saul Pasternak - Retired attorney and current director of Richdale Manor. One of Taryn's dads and Maz's boss. Looks like Sam Waterston in *Grace and Frankie*.

Jerry McHale - Retired family practice physician and current volunteer librarian. Taryn's other dad. Also volunteers with adoption and surrogacy agencies.

Sofia Vargas - Retired restauranteur. Maz's neighbor to the east, she started Taqueria Vargas with Ricky's grandfather. Married Ricky's Uncle Ramon (now deceased) after her first husband died and is therefore *Tia* to Ricky and the rest of the (large) Vargas clan. Still makes a mean tres leches cake.

Patrice DeHaven - Adjunct professor of parapsychology at Richdale University. Maz's neighbor to the west. Also owns Strings and Stones, a combination occult supply and knitting shop on Ghost's Main Street.

Haley Isaksen - Baker. Co-owns Isaksen's Bakery with her brother Jae-Seong. Taryn's girlfriend. Jerry McHale arranged her adoption by the Isaksens.

Jae-Seong Isaksen - Baker. Co-owns Isaksen's Bakery with his sister Haley. Jerry McHale arranged his adoption by the Isaksens.

Kamilla Umar - Sheriff's deputy, stationed in Ghost.

Liam Frost (formerly Guillermo Hernández) - Sofia's grandson and only living blood relative. Anglicized his first name and took his stepfather's surname when his mother remarried after his father's early death. Currently attending Harvard (financed out-of-pocket by Sofia).

Ziv Harcourt - Fictional PI. Lead character in Avi's best-selling Harcourt and Corchran thriller series.

Gabriel Corchran - Fictional reformed master thief. Secondary lead in Avi's Harcourt and Corchran thriller series.

Marguerite Windflower (aka Peg Clapp) - Psychic counselor and owner of a new age shop in Sarasota, Florida. Technically not a Ghost resident, but offers phone and online assistance for supernatural phenomena.

Hootie - Marguerite's ghost companion.

Carson Clemenson - Former real estate agent, current prison inmate. Avi's cousin; stole his work and is responsible for his death. Thwarted by Maz and Avi in *Ghostridden*.

The Vargas clan (so far)

Maria - Ricky's mother (goes by Mami); runs Taqueria Vargas with her husband, Danilo.

Danilo - Ricky's father (goes by Papi); runs Taqueria Vargas with his wife, Maria.

Felicia - Ricky's sister; high school senior who also works at Taqueria Vargas.

Nando - Ricky's cousin; co-owner of Transitions Transportation with his best friend Keegan.

Yaz - Ricky's cousin; works in dispatch at the Richdale sheriff's department.

The Richdale family (all deceased)

Josiah Richdale - Established Richdale Manor after making his fortune selling mining equipment to forty-niners during the California gold rush and moving to Oregon.

Thaddeus Richdale - Josiah's son and heir. Convinced his father had hidden the better part of his fortune from him; became obsessed with finding a way to reach "beyond the veil" and shake the information from Josiah's spirit.

Frances Richdale - Thaddeus's wife. *So* over the spiritualism crap.

Thaddeus and Frances's children - Jasper, Daisy, Iris, Violet, and the twins—Cornelius and Caroline.

Notable spots in Ghost (real and virtual)

Iris Lane (north) from east to west):

- Sofia's yellow two-story farmhouse
- Maz's Queen Anne beauty
- Patrice's Craftsman bungalow

Iris Lane (south)

- Richdale Manor grounds, with a footprint nearly as large as the rest of Ghost

Main Street

- Taqueria Vargas - restaurant owned by Ricky's family
- Isaksen's Bakery - bakery owned by Haley and Jae-Seong Isaksen

- Strings and Stones - formerly a separate occult supply and knitting shop, combined into one by Patrice DeHaven when she took them over from her relatives

- Ghost Library - run on a volunteer basis by Jerry McHale; open Tuesdays, Saturdays, and by appointment

- A pub (currently unnamed)

Richdale Manor House

- Document room containing the Richdale family archives (Maz's work area)

- Director's office (occupied by Saul Pasternak)

- Publicly accessible areas (ballrooms, dining rooms, gardens, available for rent for events)

- Historically preserved rooms (viewable on official tours)

- Gift shop

- Overly large parking lot

- Family graveyard

Elsewhere

- Jenkins House B & B

- Boos News newspaper office

- Ghostline (town online chatroom)

CHAPTER ONE

"What?" My arm jerked, but luckily the tea that slopped over the rim of my mug hit my jeans, not my laptop. "Crap, that's hot."

"Sorry." Avi, my housemate, waved his hand and a napkin wafted through the air and settled on my thigh over the spill. "I didn't think that suggestion would cause a spit-take."

I blotted the wet spot on my jeans and scowled in his direction. He was standing in front of the window, which meant I took in the lanky, brown-haired man in a shapeless cardigan as well as the view of my neighbor's house that I could see through him. Over the last month, Avi's presence had gotten a little more solid, but he was still mostly transparent.

Because Avi was a ghost, the only one here in Ghost, Oregon. Most of the town's residents would give an arm, leg, or first-born child to catch the briefest glimpse of a spirit. I had never had that ambition myself, yet here I was—the town's newest arrival, actually sharing living space with one.

Which… wasn't as alarming as it sounded. Avi, who, under the pen name Jake Fields, had been one of the most successful thriller writers of this century, and was surprisingly good company.

Except when he nearly made me spew hot tea all over my laptop.

"Not a spit-take, thank goodness. Just a slosh-and-gosh." I crumpled the wet napkin and set it on the table next to my mug. "And my jeans took one for the team."

"Clearly not for the first time," Avi murmured.

"What's that supposed to mean?"

"Oh, nothing, nothing. Let's get back to your previous overreaction."

"I didn't overreact."

He lifted an eyebrow above the rim of his wire-framed glasses. "Your jeans would beg to differ."

"I'm sorry, but what did you expect after that comment? You told me to use your money to buy a car. I can't do that!"

"The money isn't mine anymore, Maz. It's yours." Avi's tone implied that he was being completely reasonable, and I was being ridiculous. "Considering I'm dead and all. That's how inheritance works."

"I didn't inherit this place from you. I inherited it from Uncle Oren." Technically, Oren wasn't my uncle. He was my mother's second cousin once removed, and I'd never even heard his name until Taryn called to let me know I was his sole beneficiary.

"Yes," Avi said patiently, "since I left everything to him, you're, shall we say, my heir once removed? It still counts."

I poked at my keyboard, frowning. "Except usually people don't inherit from somebody who's still around."

"Technically, I'm not still around. Not to anybody except you." His gaze cut to his feet, and he smiled fondly at my cat, Gilgamesh. "Well, you and Gil."

Gil twined around Avi's ankles as though they were corporeal, which, to Gil, they might be. Who knew? Certainly not Avi or me. As far as his life—or rather, his afterlife—was concerned, we were still in the discovery process.

"Besides," Avi continued, "getting new wheels for you is totally selfish on my part. If your car breaks down and you crash, what will happen to me and the house?"

I squinted up at him, his body not blocking the sun streaming in through the window at all. "That's a little dark, don't you think?"

He shrugged. "What can I say? Who better than a ghost to snark about death?"

"I suppose that's fair." That reminded me that I should probably make a will of my own, now that I had actual—and significant—assets. "At the very least, Gil would need to hijack somebody else to supply him with tuna and kibble."

"Are you talking to yourself, Gil, or Avi?" Taryn Pasternak-McHale, my friend and attorney, wandered out of the butler's pantry, holding a bagel.

"Avi," I muttered, trying to make sense of the garbled text on the laptop screen.

"I'm guessing from your scowl that either he's telling you that you're being ridiculous about your inheritance, or whatever is on your laptop is worse than usual."

"Both." I shot a glare at her over my shoulder. "Why are you mooching bagels from my pantry, anyway? Your girlfriend literally owns a bakery."

"Co-owns, and they don't serve bagels. Yet." She grinned as she opened the refrigerator and rummaged around until she found the cream cheese. "I'm conducting market research for their expanded product line, so thank you for your service."

"Any time."

She peered at me as she slathered cream cheese on her bagel. "Maz, I could dry my hair with that tone." When I just grunted, she set the cream cheese on the counter and sauntered over to the table to peer over my shoulder. "Is this one of the ghostwriting gigs you picked up from Ghostline?"

"Yes." I looked up at her. Her brown skin glowed in the sunlight spilling in through the turret windows that surrounded the table, and she was wearing her long locs down her back today rather than in her usual business braided crown. "I appreciate you posting my credentials there. I really do." For an online town chat room for a place as small as Ghost, the post had generated a surprising number of jobs for me. "And this contract pays really well. It's just frustrating."

She leaned closer, scattering a few bagel crumbs on my shoulder. "What's it for?"

"Rewriting online help for a geography game app. Their launch date is looming and the first version was—"

"Unhelpful?"

I snorted. "You could say that. I'm pretty sure they just pointed generative AI at their wireframe documentation and called it good."

"I take it that it wasn't." She took a bite of bagel. "Good, that is."

"Not if you expected, you know, actual help. Plus, whatever engine they used had huge problems recognizing images, which is kind of an issue for a game that's literally about the shapes of countries. Slovenia was tagged as a rooster, Belize as a microwave oven, and Italy as—wait for it—a kinky boot." She and Avi both laughed, but I just shook my head. "AI is the tool of the devil."

"So what was Avi saying to you?"

I glanced at Avi, who was leaning on the air in the vicinity of the wall. "He wants me to use the Jake Fields royalties to buy myself a car, of all things."

"He's got a point." She frowned down at her bagel and walked back to the counter to plaster it with more cream cheese. "Your car looks like it's held together by coat hangers, rust, and desperation. It's older than you are by at least a dozen years."

I squinted one eye. "It's a classic?"

"It's one step from a wreck," Avi said. "Even you call it a beater. Stop being so stubborn and take the money already."

I hunched over the laptop. "You didn't complain when Ricky refused payment for maintaining the house for a decade. This is no different."

In fact, when I'd made the offer, Ricky—whom I hoped might someday transition from *friend* to *boyfriend*—had been so insulted I was afraid he'd stop speaking to me. Luckily, Ricky wasn't nearly the touchy diva that my last boyfriend had been, and the awkwardness had passed quickly.

Taryn, finished with her bagel, licked cream cheese off her fingers. "I'm guessing Avi just told you to take the money."

"Yes," I grumbled. "But it doesn't feel right to use it for something like that. It's not like Avi can drive a car."

"Look, Maz, while it's admirable that you want to share with Avi, there are some things that aren't possible. Ghosts don't have a credit rating or investment accounts, and they certainly can't stand in line at the DMV." She paused. "At least, not that I know of."

In an attempt to get them both off my back, I deflected. "This is a new look for the office, isn't it? The hair, the clothes." Taryn favored jewel-toned pantsuits in raw silk when she was in no-nonsense attorney mode, and though she had her usual Doc Martens on her feet, she was wearing a white linen camp shirt untucked over black knit pants today. "Instituting casual Wednesday?"

She shook her head, her locs swinging behind her and pattering against my arm. "I've only got two official things to do, and then I'm off for the rest of the day." She eyed the damp spot on my thigh. "What's your excuse?"

"I'm barred from the Manor for the next two days." When her brows rose, I said, "A Eugene company booked the Manor for business development nonsense, and the staff is cordially not invited to remain on the premises."

"Oh right. Which reminds me that Pop's taking advantage of the situation and dragging Dad up to Victoria for the weekend." Taryn's dad, Saul Pasternak, was my boss at Richdale Manor, Ghost's answer to the Winchester Mystery House. "Dad wanted me to let you know he wouldn't be back until Monday, so you could take Friday off, too."

"He did, huh? So why didn't you?"

"I forgot," she said, not abashed in the least. But then her face clouded. "Dad was happy enough with the venue rental fees, but I think the company could have at least catered their food locally. They're bringing it all in from Eugene, even the morning pastries. The job would have been a good bump for Isaksen's."

I swiveled in my chair to look up at her. "Is Isaksen's hurting for business?"

"Eh." She waggled one hand. "Yes and no. More is always better, within reason, anyway. Haley and I are heading into Florence to try to drum up some commercial clients for them. The lack of tourism here in town is still a problem generally, and once bookings at Jenkins House dried up, they lost their biggest local bulk order."

"Jenkins House?" I still hadn't visited the place, although it was on my to-do list. Other than my house, it was the only example of Uncle Oren's work in town. Since I'd never met the man who was Avi's lover and my own benefactor, I was curious. "That's the B & B, right?"

"It was. The couple who owned it have decided to move on."

"Rats," I muttered.

"Belay that thought, because one of my tasks today is conveying the title for the place to the previous owners' relatives." She held up both hands, fingers crossed. "With luck, they'll decide to reopen and avail themselves of Jae-Seong's fabulous pastries again. But even if they do, Isaksen's still needs to diversify. Hence today's trip to the coast."

"Can Jae-Seong manage the bakery without Haley?"

She shrugged. "It's just for the day, and the baking's already done. They've got a couple of part-timers who can cover service."

"Let me guess." I leaned back in my chair and crossed my arms. "Could those part-timers be more of Ricky's cousins?" I'd never been able to tie Ricky down to a final count, but his cousins were *everywhere*.

"I'll never tell." She smirked. "Maybe you should ask him."

"Maybe I will. He'll be here later." My neck prickled at the thought of seeing him again, of spending time with him again.

My mandatory Manor moratorium was good for that, at least. "I'm helping him set out vegetable starts in Sofia's garden today."

"Sheesh." Taryn rolled her eyes. "Watching the two of you tiptoe around each other is like watching glaciers migrate."

My eyebrows snapped together. "Hey! That's not fair. Ricky's important. I don't want to screw this up."

"Okay. I guess I can accept that." Her expression turned calculating, almost sly. "You've got five days free. Seems like a perfect time to move that glacier a little farther down the mountain."

I looked out the window at the back of Sofia's scarecrow. "You really need to work on your metaphors."

Taryn studied me, eyes narrowed. "You're not going to do it, are you?"

"Do what?" I suspected my attempt at nonchalance was a total failure.

"Take Friday off."

"It's either that or spend all day on these stupid help files, and believe me, a few hours at a time is all I can handle."

Taryn spread her hands. "Then why take the jobs? It's not like you need the money now. Or are you saying I didn't negotiate appropriate compensation for you when Dad offered you the Manor job?"

"Of course not! But even if you hadn't, it wouldn't have mattered. The work over there is fascinating."

Fascinating was an understatement. The Richdale family cast a vast shadow over the area. The town of Ghost wouldn't exist if not for them, nor would nearby Richdale or Richdale University. My neighbor, Patrice DeHaven, taught paranormal studies there when she wasn't lurking inside her house in self-imposed introvert seclusion.

In the last half of his life, Thaddeus Richdale's time, money, and energy had all been devoted to his quest to reach beyond the veil. Not because he was a particularly spiritual person, you understand. No, he just wanted to shake down Josiah, his departed father, for the location of the fortune Thaddeus was convinced Josiah had hidden from him.

Saul had hired me to organize Thaddeus's papers, and I was finally making some progress. This event couldn't have come at a worse time, but the Manor needed the rental fees, so I had to deal.

Both Taryn and Avi were looking down at me, shaking their heads as though I'd disappointed them hugely. Gil, the traitor, had his back to me, ears tilted back, only the tip of his ginger tail twitching.

"Stop it. Both of you." I leaned sideways, the better to glare at Gil. "You too." I sighed. "Oh, fine. I'll *think* about taking Friday off."

Taryn grinned. "That's all I ask."

The ping of an incoming text emanated from the oversized leather purse Taryn had slung on the counter when she'd arrived.

"That'll be Haley. I need to get moving. Which brings me to my second task of the day."

She strode over to her bag and extracted two envelopes, one a thick eight by ten manila and the other a standard business size with some kind of logo where the return address should be. She slapped the bigger one on the counter.

"What's that?"

"The court documents from the settled lawsuits, as well as an updated contract from Avi's publisher for his last book." She tapped two fingers on the clasp. "They'll be returning the advance, too."

Avi surged forward, his feet not touching the floor. "They did? I didn't expect that."

I gestured to where Avi was standing to peer down at the envelope. "Avi says he didn't expect to get the advance back."

Taryn gave me a pitying look. "Maz. *Avi* didn't get the advance. As the person who turned in the manuscript, *you* did.

Although frankly?" She faced in the direction I'd indicated. "Avi, your publisher was so ecstatic to get it, I think your agent could have asked for double and they'd have come through." She grinned. "Have I told you how much I *like* her?"

Avi and I both said, "Several times."

Taryn ignored me, still directing her comments toward Avi's general location. "I made sure that she negotiated to send all the editor's notes here to Maz."

"Me? Why?"

She rolled her eyes. "Don't be dense, Maz. So Avi can do the edits, of course. Nobody has to know they're being done by a ghost."

"But I can't interact with a computer," Avi said. "Remember last week when I crashed your laptop?"

I winced. "Right." That had been a near disaster, but I'd only lost an hour or so of work on those lousy help files, so it could definitely have been worse. "Maybe you could use dictation software or something."

Avi dipped his chin and glared at me over his glasses. "Exactly how would I do that, Maz? You're the only person, place, or thing who can hear my voice."

"Oh, yeah. I guess that would be a problem. Don't worry. We'll figure something out."

"And this"—Taryn flourished the smaller envelope and waggled it in the air until I took it—"is for you." She grabbed her bag. "Gotta go." She turned and power-walked out of the room.

I opened the envelope warily and peeked inside. My eyes widened, and I threw it onto the counter where it skidded to the edge and fell to the floor.

"Taryn!" I stormed out of the kitchen and planted myself in the family room just as she reached the front door. "Why the *hell* did you just hand me a check for a hundred and twenty-five grand?"

CHAPTER TWO

Taryn's hand fell from the doorknob, and she turned with a sigh. "Maz Amani, you are the hardest person in the world to give money to. Anybody else would be thrilled."

"I bet anybody else would still want to know what the money was for."

"You'd be surprised. Most would just take it and run." She moved to the bottom of the staircase and set her bag on the bottom step. "Do you remember when we first met?"

"Of course."

"The day after you moved in, we sat on these stairs and you asked me whether Oren's estate included any cash. At that time, because of the lawsuits, it didn't. Now the lawsuits are settled, so why are you hesitant to take the proceeds?"

"Because before, I didn't know Avi was here. It feels wrong to use money that he earned on things that have nothing to do with him."

"Hmmm." Her eyes flicked to the family room door and the kitchen archway beyond. "Is Avi nearby?"

"Still in the kitchen, as far as I know. He didn't follow me, anyway."

With a tiny nod, she beckoned me forward, lowering her voice. "Did anyone tell you the results of Carson's arrest?"

"I didn't ask." Having somebody wave a gun in your face was best forgotten as soon as possible.

She laid a hand on my arm, but focused on my shoulder instead of my face. "Carson took a plea."

"A plea," I said woodenly. "Great."

"He got the maximum jail time for the copyright infringement and the threat with a deadly weapon charges. Five years each, to be served consecutively."

"He should have been convicted for murdering Avi," I muttered.

"Yeah, well, I'm sorry about that, but the DA was afraid the jury wouldn't buy causality between the attack and Avi's death." She pursed her lips and exhaled. "The publisher pushed for the maximum fine on the copyright case and got it. They kept half, because of course they did, but Avi's contract specified a 50% share of any incidental income accrued from his work, hence your check."

I frowned down at her. "Carson might have been a real estate agent, but you can't tell me he had two hundred and fifty thousand dollars just lying around."

She shrugged. "He had to liquidate most of his assets, which he wasn't happy about. But if he hadn't agreed, the DA threatened to put Avi's assault back on the table, although without the murder charge because of said causality issue."

I huffed out a breath. "I will never understand the legal system."

"What can I say? Legal doesn't always equate to fair." She patted my arm once and picked up her bag. "Are you going to cash that check?"

I glanced over my shoulder. Still no sign of Avi. "It's not mine."

"Look." She hitched her bag onto her shoulder. "I can sort of see your point about the royalties, although I think you need to get over it. But this is different. Think of it as a… a finder's fee."

"Finder's fee?"

"Yes. If it weren't for you, Avi's last book would have remained lost, maybe forever, possibly destroyed. His reputation had been tarnished by Carson's actions, but you've set its redemption in motion. You faced the barrel of a gun for his sake, Maz." She shivered, blinking rapidly. "You've *earned* this, and I'm sure Avi feels the same way. So just take the fricking money and buy a car, okay?"

She didn't wait for my answer this time, just swept out the door, closing it behind her with a decisive *click*.

"A finder's fee. Sure. Whatever."

I wandered into the library and watched from the turret windows as she marched down my walk and climbed into her Prius. Although I waited, scanning the street while she drove away, there was no sign of Ricky yet. He'd told me he had a couple of stops to make first, so—

"She's right, you know."

I screeched and stumbled away from the window, banging my hip on the edge of the desk in the process.

"Jeez, Avi. Don't sneak up on me like that."

He chuckled as he drifted over and sat on the window seat. Well, on-ish. He had one leg tucked underneath him, but his butt was floating about an inch above the cushion. Gil hopped up next to him and zeroed in on a crested jay who was squawking away on the porch railing.

"You live with a ghost, Maz. Surely you should be used to jump scares by now."

"I suppose." I dropped onto the curve of the window seat next to the desk. "Did you, um, hear what Taryn said about Carson?"

He nodded. "I did."

"Does it bother you? That he wasn't charged with your murder?"

"Honestly?" He lifted one shoulder and reached out to stroke Gil's back, making his fur lift along his spine as though Avi's palm were infused with static electricity. Which, for all we knew, it was. "Not as much as it probably should."

I glared out the window at the pansies nodding along the edge of the walk, at the shadows cast on the neatly trimmed lawn by the maple leaves, at the porch swing swaying in the breeze. Avi had never had the chance to enjoy that with Oren. All because of Carson.

"It sure as hell bothers me."

"Don't misunderstand. I'm still angry. Incandescently so."

Since a stack of unpaid bills on the desk started to stir, I knew he was telling the truth about that. Avi's rage tended to express itself with airborne paper goods.

"However," he said, "my anger is more on Oren's behalf. Yes, I was robbed of time we could have spent together, but I wasn't aware of its passage. I was"—he made a circular motion with one hand—"elsewhere. But Oren had to live through those years without me, without *us*. From what you've told me, he never recovered from the loss, not even to return here, to this town, to this house." His expression hardened. "That, I can never forgive."

"Yeah, I get that. But—"

"But." He held up one finger. "*But*. I probably know more about Carson than anybody except his revolting spiritual twin."

I lifted a brow. "I take it you mean Liam? Sofia's grandson?"

"The same."

"Ricky calls their relationship the Young Assholes of America bond."

Avi snorted. "Apt. Anyway, I know that the best way to punish Carson is to deprive him of what he values most. His possessions. His reputation." He fixed me with a stare. "His money. So will you do me a favor, Maz?"

The intensity of Avi's gaze practically shoved me against the window. "S-sure, Avi. Anything."

"Cash that check and *take his fucking money*."

I winced. *Crap.* I'd just painted myself into a proverbial corner, hadn't I? I probably shouldn't be surprised. As Jake Fields, Avi knew how to craft a good plot twist, not to mention lay a mean trap for poor, unsuspecting ghostwriters.

Emphasis on the *poor*, so maybe I needed to stop fighting this so hard.

"Fine. I'll cash the check." I glared at him from under lowered brows. "But I won't like it."

He flashed a grin. "I can live with that. Or rather, not live, but you know what I mean. We're making *excellent* progress here. Now." He stood up and crossed the turret to loom over me. "I want you to listen to me, Maz. And I mean really listen. Not only listen, but *hear* me."

I swallowed. "Okay."

His eyebrows shot down and the bills rose from the desk next to me, rustling in the air. "Stop being such an idiot!"

"Beg pardon?"

"Because of what Carson did, this house never had the chance to become a home."

"But you grew up here. It was already your home."

"It was not. It was simply the house I'd inherited from my parents. A beautiful house. A house that Oren and I showered with time, money, and his incredible talent. But still just a house. It hadn't crossed that last line because I was waiting for him. Waiting for Oren."

His face shuttered for an instant, and I knew what he was thinking. He was still waiting for Oren, and maybe always would.

Avi took a breath and met my gaze. "Then you came. You didn't freak out when you found out you were sharing the space with a ghost."

"I wouldn't go *that* far." I had freaked out pretty significantly.

A smile glimmered on his lips. "Well, only at first. But then you *accepted* me. *Involved* me. *Partnered* with me, in a way. You made the attic my personal space."

"To be fair, Ricky helped with that, as did the guys from Transitions Transportation."

He waved a hand. "It was your idea, even if you didn't personally relocate everything." His gaze caught on his left hand which was still in the air. "You gave something to me that I would never have gotten should anybody else have inherited this place and Oren's things." He touched the wedding band gently. "You gave me my husband."

I took a shaky breath, forcing air into my leaden lungs. Because the evidence of Oren's plans for a surprise Canadian wedding, one that Avi hadn't lived to see, still hurt.

Not for the first time since I'd gotten that call from Taryn telling me I'd inherited this house, I wished I'd known about the bequest before it was too late. Maybe Oren and I could have helped each other, sustained each other through the grief of his loss of Avi and my loss of my parents. At the very least, neither of us would have been alone.

"Any decent person would have done the same."

Avi chuckled. "In case you hadn't noticed, decency isn't always the default setting for our fellow humans."

"I guess not. But I still think we have the right to expect it."

"Trust, but verify, Maz. When it comes to decency, trust, but verify." His gaze slid away from me. "So, you claim this is our house now, correct? Our home?"

I narrowed my eyes, because when Avi had used that tone a few minutes ago, I'd walked right into a trap. "Yeeaahh."

"That means I need to contribute, too."

"Hey, you're a great housemate. Thanks to your dustbusting superpowers, we'll never need to vacuum or hire a cleaning service. Heck, you even disappear Gil's fur." I shuddered at the image of a vast, spectral fur ball. "And it's not like you're going to drink the last of the OJ or leave your underwear on the bathroom floor. Besides, you contributed the whole freaking house. You're covered."

His chin firmed in that way I was starting to recognize: Avi in stubborn mode. He pointed to the bills that were still suspended over the desk. "The top bill on that stack is for the security system, which you seem to be paying in installments. Out of your ghostwriting earnings and Manor salary."

I shifted uneasily. I hadn't intended for him to see that. Who knew ghosts could be nosy? "So?"

"You can't say *that's* not to my benefit. I want people breaking in here even less than you do, because there's nothing I could do to them, not even confront them."

I glanced at the hovering bills. "Well, you could give them one hell of a paper cut."

"I'm serious, Maz. The royalty money is finally there now. Use it."

"I'll… consider it." He narrowed his eyes, and I held my hands up to ward off the glare. "Fine. I'll use it to pay for the security system."

"And other things, too. Oregon property taxes are no joke, and an old house like this needs constant upkeep, not to mention the grounds. Ricky did it for years for no compensation, but he's not allowed to do that anymore. If he does the work, he takes the cash." He folded his arms. "Tell him that."

I held up my hands, palms out. "Nope. Not a chance. Hitting him with a cease-and-desist for future work would go over just as well as offering him payment for services already rendered." After my failed attempt to pay Ricky for his work, I'd figured out that his love language was acts of service. Offering him something as impersonal as cash in exchange was the equivalent of rejecting his care and affection. "I'd prefer not to scuttle our friendship over a battle I already lost."

"Friendship?" He waggled his eyebrows. "Are you sure you don't want… more?"

"Whether I do or not is immaterial."

"I disagree. It's very material." His gaze swept from my worn sneakers, up my faded jeans and over my faded Talking Heads T-shirt. "As in *those* materials. The new tea stain might actually be an improvement. Perhaps you should invest in some new clothes."

"Hey!" I plucked at the T's hem. "This is sheer practicality. Since I'm helping Ricky with Sofia's garden today, I fully expect to be covered in dirt and sweat by the end of the afternoon. I didn't want to ruin my nicer clothes."

Leaning forward, he clasped his hands behind his back— which was really weird because I could see through him to his hands, but also see through his hands. "So you do have nicer clothes?"

"I have perfectly serviceable clothes."

"Maz. Please. You can hardly expect to woo Ricky when you look more raggedy than the scarecrow in Sofia's garden."

"That's not hard. Sofia's scarecrow has serious style."

He chuckled and stopped looming over me. "That it does."

I cocked my head. "You've seen it? It doesn't look old enough to have been around ten years ago."

"It wasn't. Since I can't go outside, I've only seen it from above, but I've got a good view from the attic window."

I heaved a relieved sigh. The scarecrow was a near perfect representation of Carson in effigy, and Avi didn't need the reminder. Maybe I could ask Ricky to replace it with something less identifiable.

"Have you tried it? Going out into the backyard since I got here? I mean, that's part of this... this domain."

"Domain?" Avi lifted an eyebrow. "Really?"

I flung my arms out. "I don't know. But it's part of what you owned, you and Oren. You, um, died in the backyard."

Avi's gaze drifted to the window. "And maybe that's why I can't go there again."

"Ah." For a moment, I watched Avi gazing out the window. "Do you... Is that a choice? I mean, do you *want* to go outside, go somewhere other than here in the house, and you're just not able to?"

He shrugged one shoulder. "I don't know. Maybe." Then he gave me a sidelong glance. "On the other hand, I *do* go somewhere else. I just don't know where that somewhere is. Like I said. Elsewhere. Maybe it's nowhere." He held his hands out, studying them as he turned them palm up, palm down, palm up again. "Maybe someday, I'll be elsewhere all the time."

My belly clenched, and I bunched my fists on my knees. "You mean you might die?"

He gave me a look. "Don't make me state the obvious."

I winced. "Sorry."

"I do have another question." When I nodded and made a go-ahead motion with one hand, he said, "When I speak to you, if your other friends are present, you tell them I've spoken, and often what I've said, verbatim. Why?"

"Because you're their dream come true." I held my palms out to him. "An honest to goodness ghost here in town, something they've been waiting for their entire lives."

"Yes, but if what I say embarrasses you, why tell them exactly what I say? They can't hear me, so they'd never know the difference."

"No. But you would."

"I wouldn't mind." He gave me a sly, tightlipped smile. "I might haunt you, Maz, but I don't want you to be uncomfortable."

"You don't *haunt* me. We share a house. As far as... as translating for you?" I inhaled slowly and then let out my breath in a rush. "I guess it's the same way I approach my job. As a ghostwriter, my duty is to convey the author's story in the way that best delivers their intent, not to alter it based on what I *think* their story should be or skew it for my own benefit."

He leaned forward with that laser-intent gaze again. "What he said bothered you, didn't it? Carson. When he said you stole from other writers."

I looked away and shrugged. "He's a delusional homicidal plagiarist. Why should what he says bother me?"

"It shouldn't. But it does." He paused, lips parted. "Wait a minute." He straightened so quickly he floated a foot off the ground. The bills, on the other hand, dropped to the desktop. "*That's* why."

CHAPTER THREE

I eyed Avi while I snaked an arm out and opened the nearest desk drawer to sweep the bills inside, away from prying ghosts with aerial talents. "That's why what?"

"Why you refuse to touch the royalty money. Why you haven't moved in."

"It's not *the* royalty money, Avi. It's *your* royalty money. And, hey." I jabbed my finger toward the floor. "I've moved in. I sleep in the primary bedroom. My car's parked in the garage. My cat's litter box is in the mudroom, his food dishes are in the kitchen, and his toys are scattered all over the house from hell to breakfast."

"That's exactly my point. Other than the clothes you claim are serviceable, the car that hardly qualifies as transportation, the laptop which is about as workmanlike as you can get, and the bare minimum of grooming supplies, your cat has more *personal* items here than you do."

"I— Wait." Had I let my scruff get too scruffy? "Do you think I need more grooming supplies?"

He folded his arms, the toe of one foot tapping soundlessly. "Would you buy them with the royalty money if I said yes?"

"Well..." I scratched the back of my head. Should I get my hair trimmed? My curls reached past my shoulders now. "Doesn't that seem like an inappropriate use of funds?"

"Oh, for the love of—" He flung his hands in the air and float-marched to the middle of the room before turning to face me. "Look at this library."

Lowering my eyebrows, I glanced around the room. "Yeah. It's amazing. I thought so the first time I saw it."

"We had that desk custom built by a local woodworker."

I ran my hand along its gleaming oak top. "They did a fantastic job."

"Yet the only thing you use it for is to hide your bills." He pointed at me when I grimaced. "Yeah, don't think I missed that little maneuver."

"Sorry." I peeked up at him, caught the exasperated look on his face, and switched to studying my frayed sneaker laces. "The desk really is beautiful."

"Then tell me." He hunkered down in front of me and looked up into my face. "Why do you always set up your laptop on the table and work in the kitchen? Are you still traumatized by that tantrum I threw in here before I understood what was going on? Because you know I didn't do it on purpose. I'll never forgive myself if that's given you an aversion to the room."

That brought my head up with a snap. "No! I don't blame you for that. And if any room should traumatize me, it should be the kitchen, since that's where I was, you know, held at gunpoint."

"Then why? Why won't you work in here?"

I dropped my head again. "Because this was your office," I mumbled.

He cupped a hand behind his ear. "What was that?"

"I *said* this was *your office*." I didn't shout. Almost. But then my shoulders fell and I gazed out the window so I couldn't see the hurt in his eyes—or the pattern of the rug through his body. My voice dropped to nearly inaudible. "And this was where it happened."

"Maz." Avi's words matched my vocal level. "I didn't die here."

I looked up at him. "No. But if you hadn't been attacked here, while you were working at *this*"—I jabbed my finger against the desktop—"desk, you'd never have died in the backyard."

He scrunched up his face, making his glasses lift off his nose, and stood up with a sigh. "Evidently, both of us need to work on reclaiming spaces that trigger us. Maybe we can help each other do that. Deal?"

We couldn't shake hands, so I stood and faced him, once again noting that we were exactly the same height. I nodded. "Deal."

He returned the nod. "Cool. So if we ever find a way for me to step outside, you can coach me through the yard. In the meantime, let me assist you in staking your claim inside the house. You don't need to keep it as a shrine to Oren and me."

"It's not a shrine." I pointedly did *not* stare at the shelf that held all of Avi's Jake Fields books. "While the house may be mine legally because of those pesky laws that prevent the deceased from owning property, I share it with you. You should have some say."

His smile was a little evil. "Then here's my say." He leaned forward. "If you have to work up the gumption to use the royalty money over time, I can respect that. But meanwhile, at least hang up a photograph or two. Stick your favorite mugs in the kitchen cabinets. Put your own books on the shelves. *Move in.*"

"Well." I picked at a loose thread on my jeans. "There's a thing."

He lifted an eyebrow. "A thing? What kind of thing?"

"The kind of thing where my conflict avoidance kicks in and makes me want to barricade myself in a blanket fort to stress-eat Sofia's tres leches cake."

"While I would take any excuse to gobble up Sofia's cake, would you care to be more specific about the conflict in question?"

"Specifically, the conflict with my ex." I sank down the onto window seat, drew one knee up and clasped my hands around my shin. "In order to get the rest of my belongings—not that there are many of them, mind you—I have to face Greg again. The boxes are all in his condo."

"Ah." He shoved his hands in his cardigan pockets, making the front hem dip, and shrugged. "I'd offer to accompany you when you confront him, except for one tiny issue."

"You can't leave the house."

His eyebrows rose, his eyes widening in exaggerated shock. "I'd forgotten about that."

"There's another problem?"

"Yes." He smirked at me. "Can't you guess?"

I shook my head, rolling my eyes. "I know I'm going to regret this. What?"

"Because I wouldn't be caught dead in your car."

I turned away as he snickered. "Are all ghosts smartasses, or is that just you?"

"If we ever find another one, we can ask."

I caught a glimpse of chrome and shiny gray paint beyond the maple leaves. *Ricky*.

Avi stood behind my shoulder as Ricky got out of his truck. "I have vague recollections of hearing a lawn mower and seeing him weeding the flower beds. But I don't know if that's from before or since." He smiled wanly as Ricky got out of the truck and headed up the walk. "He took care of the lawn back then too, you see, so maybe I'm remembering those times instead."

I thought about this as Ricky neared the porch. He caught sight of me in the window and he lifted one hand in greeting, his smile dawning, which sent its usual thrill down my spine.

Ricky's smile was deadly.

He paused for a moment, his smile fading, then shook his head and mounted the steps.

"You said you promised Oren to wait here, in the house. Maybe you needed somebody to *be* in the house before you could, er, manifest. Nobody had been inside since Saul locked everything down after the funeral."

Avi shrugged again. "I must have been able to do *something*." He gestured to the room. "No dust."

"Right. And sawdust in the keyholes."

The door opened and Ricky called, "Maz?"

"Come on in. We're in the library."

I turned to meet him, but Gil beat me to it, greeting Ricky with an imperative *mrrow* at the library's open french doors. He leaned down to skritch Gil between the ears.

"Hey, Gil."

He stood when I reached the edge of the rug.

"Hey," I said.

"Hey," he replied.

My smile must have been absolutely ludicrous because behind me, Avi snorted and muttered something that sounded suspiciously like *glaciers*.

Ricky peered over my shoulder. "Is, um, Avi here?"

I nodded. "He's over by the windows. He was standing a little behind me when you pulled up and he's still there."

I cut a glance over my shoulder at him and mouthed *asshole*. Avi just chuckled, shaking his head.

Ricky pulled his lower lip between his teeth. "I'm not sure, but I *think* I may have caught a glimpse of him."

Avi was by my side as though he'd teleported. "He saw me? So maybe other people could see me?"

"Avi is... really excited by that possibility." I jerked a thumb at where Avi stood at my shoulder. "He moved."

"Can he see me now?" Avi's voice was trembling as he edged forward. "Does he know I'm standing right in front of him?"

"He, um, wants to know if you can still see him."

"Sorry." Ricky spread his hands, one of which passed through Avi's cardigan sleeve. "Nada."

Avi seemed to deflate. "I suppose it was too much to ask."

"What exactly did you see?" I asked Ricky.

"I thought I saw someone next to you, but it was just a hint, like a reflection, but on the other side of the window?" He grimaced. "I didn't mean to get anybody's hopes up."

"Hey, it's still a possibility. Something to consider." I picked Gil up so he could bump his nose against Avi's shoulder, which had seemed to fade a little after his disappointment. "Although if I were you, I wouldn't mention it to Saul or Patrice yet. They might camp out on my lawn just on the off chance of a repeat sighting."

Ricky laughed and Avi managed a somewhat watery chuckle. "You're probably right." He clapped his hands and rubbed his palms together. "So. Are you ready for our gardening adventure?"

I spread my arms, putting my much-maligned outfit on display. "As you see." I shot Avi a glance. He was gazing at Gil, and although he was stroking the cat's head, he still looked dejected. Almost... forlorn. "Although Avi's been giving me grief today about my wardrobe."

Ricky's brows rose. "Why?"

"He seems to think I don't dress well enough to—"

"Woo him," Avi murmured.

I cleared my throat. "That I don't dress well."

"You're dressed fine for gardening."

I jabbed a finger in Avi's direction. "*Exactly*. Besides, I don't have the money for new clothes."

Ricky huffed a laugh. "Don't feel pressured to adopt a style you don't feel suits you, but if you wanted new clothes, you have more than enough to beef up your wardrobe."

"I don't want to waste my resources unnecessarily. Saul pays me well and I've gotten some decent-paying gigs through Ghostline, but I'm not exactly rolling in the dough."

"You could roll in it if you wanted," Avi said. "You're just being stubborn."

"I *told* you," I said through gritted teeth. "That's *your* money. Not mine."

Ricky reached out to pet Gil, who, from the sound of his purr, deeply appreciated getting attention from three people at once. "I'm guessing Avi just told you to use the money you legitimately inherited."

"I sense a certain double standard here." I pinged my narrow-eyed gaze from Avi to Ricky. "You want me to take money for something I had absolutely no hand in earning, spend it on luxuries like new clothes and a car, yet you refuse to accept a penny for an entire decade of actual, physical labor."

"A car?" Ricky's expression wouldn't have been out of place on a teenager unwrapping the latest gaming system on Christmas morning. "You're getting a new car?"

"*That's* your takeaway?" I threw up my hands. "I give up."

He hit me with pure puppy-dog eyes. "Does that mean you *are* getting a new car?"

"No, I am not getting a new car, despite Avi and Taryn nagging me about it."

"You should. What you drive barely passes for a car anymore. I worry that it'll give out on you at a bad moment."

"See?" Avi held out his palms toward Ricky. "I told you."

"Since the only place I drive anymore is from here to the Manor, which, I might add, I might stop once I find out if it's all right for me to cut across the grounds and walk, it's hardly an issue at the moment."

Ricky grinned. "We'll wear you down, eventually. And when you're ready, I can get you a good deal. One of my cousins owns a car dealership in Eugene."

"I'd expect nothing less," I said dryly. "How many cousins do you have again?"

"You can count them the next time we have a family party." Something flickered across his face and I could practically track the joy draining away from him.

"Ricky? What is it?"

He heaved a sigh. "It's just that Tia wanted to have a big party for Liam's Harvard graduation. She's been planning it for months. But then Liam told her he's got an internship starting in Manhattan the day after commencement and he can't make it home."

"Is Sofia upset?"

"She's sad. But you'll never get her to blame Liam. As far as she's concerned, he can do no wrong."

"Do you think he *doesn't* have an internship?"

"No, he's probably got one. He was always able to talk himself into anything when he put his mind to it. But because of that, I think he could have made an effort to delay his start date by a few days."

I set Gil down. "Had she already talked to the family about the party?"

"Are you kidding? She had Felicia send out save-the-date cards three months ago."

"Then you know what?" I dusted Gil's fur off my palms and headed toward the family room. "If everybody's already got the date on their calendar, let's have the party, anyway. Who cares if Liam can't be there?"

Ricky and Avi both scoffed at the same moment. "Sofia."

I paused by the kitchen archway. "Oh. I suppose that's true. Could she still enjoy herself, anyway?"

Ricky nodded slowly, his smile dawning. "She always loves being with family and friends."

"What date?"

"June first. Commencement is on May twenty-ninth. She wanted to give him time to move out of his dorm first."

"Then let's do it." A little seed of anticipation sprouted in my middle. I didn't go in for big parties as a rule, but I'd make an exception this time. In fact... "Let's make it a blowout for the whole town. Ghost might be bleeding tourism dollars, but all the more reason for the townies to band together. We can use our house and yard as overflow. Heck, Patrice would probably let us use her yard too, as long as we don't make her attend."

Ricky's big brown eyes shone as he gazed at me in what I might have described as awe if I wasn't, you know, me. "You'd do that? For Tia?"

"Of course." *And for you.* "We'll ask her today, and if she agrees, it's totally on."

I looked down at Gil, and then up at Avi. I'd been planning to take Gil over to Sofia's while Ricky and I worked on the garden, since she always seemed to enjoy his company. But today, I thought Avi needed the emotional support floof more.

"Avi, can you watch Gil while we're working?"

Avi crouched down next to my cat, who immediately bumped his forehead against Avi's knee as if it were as solid as mine. "Any time. Although I hardly think he's going to run rampant through the house."

"You have no idea. Why do you think I keep breakable things inside cabinets?"

He sank onto the floor and sat cross-legged next to the sofa. "Forewarned, eh? Don't worry. We'll be fine." Since Gil immediately settled in the cradle of Avi's legs, I decided to believe him.

Ricky and I walked through the archway into the kitchen, but I slowed at the swinging door that led to the butler's pantry when I noticed he wasn't behind me anymore. When I turned, he was standing next to the island, running a finger along its end-grain butcher block top.

"You don't need to do this, you know, Maz. I've put in Sofia's garden on my own since I was a teenager."

"Hey." I backtracked so I could stand beside him. "I want to do this. I've been looking forward to it, and not just because it's an escape from a truly aggravating ghostwriting job."

He peered up at me, his teeth denting his lower lip. "If you're sure?"

"Positive." I gestured for him to precede me through the door. "Although you might have second thoughts before we're done."

"Why would you think that?"

"Weeelll." I grabbed a hoodie off its hook in the mudroom as we passed through. "I don't exactly have a green thumb. One of my friends wrote this fabulous humorous gardening book, but when I offered to help her with planting one spring, she laughed so hard she snorted. So apparently, the idea of me in the garden was funnier than anything in a book titled *Slug Tossing*."

CHAPTER FOUR

Two hours later, I stood and arched my back with a satisfying crack. The knees of my jeans were caked with mud, as were the fingers on the gardening gloves Ricky had lent me. Granted, I hadn't done much but dig where Ricky told me and carry the pots of vegetable starts from his pickup truck, but that didn't mean I couldn't share the satisfaction of neat rows of leggy tomatoes, spiky chiles, clusters of cucumbers and melons, the leafy floofs of lettuce, cilantro, and parsley.

I eyed the scarecrow, wondering whether I could convince a few birds to dive-bomb it or do a head-poop fly-by on Avi's behalf. Sadly, I doubted it. I could rarely control my own cat, let alone random neighborhood wildlife. *Crap.*

Ricky finished watering the last row of cantaloupes and joined me at the edge of the enormous garden patch. "Thanks for the help."

"I didn't do that much. Just call me Minion."

"Still, I finished in half the time, so it's all good."

"I've been meaning to ask you." I pointed at the scarecrow. "Who made that?"

Ricky chuckled, a little evilly. "I did. Felicia helped, and so did our cousin Eliana. She's studying art at Northwest College of Arts and Sciences up in Portland."

"It's epic."

"That it is."

"Enrique?" Sofia called from her back porch. "You are finished already?"

"Yes, Tia," Ricky said. "Everything went much quicker with Maz helping. Come see your garden." He gave her a stern look. "But only to look. You're not allowed to do any work. Not even to pull a single weed. I'll take care of that for you."

"Ah, bah," she said as she made her way down the porch steps, one hand on the railing. "A little bending is good for me."

"A little bending can set off one of your episodes. Which reminds me. I refilled your prescription. It's in my truck. I'll bring it in once I've cleaned up a little." He hurried across the lawn and held out a hand to help her down the last step, grinning at her. "I wouldn't want to track mud into your nice clean house."

She patted his chest. "If you did, you would have cleaned it up, just as you always do. You take such good care of me, you and your sister and your parents, just as Guillermo would do if he could be here."

Ricky slid me a glance. "Of course." He escorted her to the edge of the garden plot. "What do you think?"

She clasped her hands under her chin. "It is lovely. And even more lovely will be what I will cook in the fall." Her crown of white braids shone in the sun as she smiled up at me. "I will make special salsa for you, Maz, for helping." She leaned forward and lowered her voice. "Spicier than what Maria serves in the restaurant. The kind just for family."

"Tia's salsa is the best," Ricky said.

"Then I look forward to it."

Sofia sighed and her smile faded. She was still looking at the garden, but I don't think she saw it—her gaze seemed distant.

"Tia? What's wrong?"

She patted Ricky's arm. "It is Guillermo."

"What about him?"

"Now that he cannot come home after his graduation, I do not know how I will get his gift to him, or the check for law school." She turned her smile back on as she faced me. "He is staying at Harvard for law school, you know."

"I didn't, but that's pretty impressive."

She chuckled. "He thought about Yale, but he said he couldn't betray Harvard that way, so he is staying."

"Can you mail everything to him?" I asked.

She shook her head. "His address is changing, but even it had not, Guillermo does not trust delivery services with such large checks. He says their employees cannot always be trusted. He has studied many cases of theft in his classes, he told me. But I can no longer do what I used to."

I exchanged a glance with Ricky, whose expression had gone suspiciously blank, so I had to ask. "What did you used to do?"

"Oh, I would give the check to Carson to take to Guillermo. He often attended real estate conferences in Boston, so they both assured me it was no trouble. But now that Carson is away, I don't know what to do."

Carson was away, all right, although ten years wasn't nearly enough, in my opinion. It should have been twenty-five to life.

"I planned to throw him a graduation party," she said to me.

"Yes, Ricky told me."

She sighed. "That would have been so perfect. His friends and family could have celebrated with him, and I could have given him the tuition check and his gift as well."

"You're giving him *more* money, Tia?"

"Bah. Money is not the important thing." She beamed. "In my scrapbooking group, I have been working on a special album for him, with many memories from his life. It is very large, though, so I am not certain how to get it to him."

Ricky draped an arm across her shoulder and gave her a sideways hug. "Don't worry, Tia. We'll figure something out."

"You are such a good boy, Enrique." She gave his chest a pat and then shook out her apron. "Now I will get you two some iced tea. You've been working hard and must be thirsty."

"You don't have to do that on my account, Sofia."

"It is no trouble. I will be back inmediatamente."

Ricky and I stood shoulder to shoulder, watching her climb the porch steps and disappear into the house.

"Let me get this straight," I said slowly. "She pays for his tuition—his *Harvard* tuition—out of pocket and he can't even be bothered to come here to pick up the check?"

"He claims he doesn't want to incur the expense of the flight. Since that would be paid by Tia too."

"Why can't she just pay the school directly? It's all electronic now, anyway."

"He says he doesn't want to bother her with bills, and she doesn't even have a credit card anymore after her last one got hit with thousands of dollars of charges from a resort in Belize."

"Damn. Did her card get stolen at the same time as that jewelry theft?"

"No. It was several years ago, and the card was never out of her possession. The number just got spoofed." He shrugged. "It happens. Saul took care of it for her, no charge. It was one of the last things he did before he retired from his law practice."

"So she pays cash for everything now?"

Ricky lowered his chin and gave me a *get real* look, and I got it.

"Ah. She doesn't have to. Because you do her grocery shopping."

"Me or my sister, although Felicia isn't eighteen yet, so there are some things she can't buy."

"Does Sofia reimburse you?"

He snorted. "I'm not going to demand money from her for trivial things."

"Right. Trivial things, like food and medicine."

It occurred to me again that I had no idea what Ricky's actual job was. He always seemed to have time to fill in at Taqueria Vargas if the restaurant was short staffed, spend an entire morning in the middle of the week planting his godmother's garden, or show up whenever hapless ghostwriters needed their locks cleared out.

Nobody knew better than I did that being self-employed meant that you could arrange your working hours to suit you, but when exactly was Ricky doing work for which he'd *get* paid? He sure wasn't accepting any money from Sofia or me.

I sucked in a breath.

"Maz?" Ricky peered up at me. "What's wrong?"

"Nothing. Nothing at all." In fact, things had just taken a turn for the awesome, because I could see how I could solve three problems at once. "We talked about holding Sofia's party whether Liam was here or not, right?"

"Yeah." He drew the word out, suspicion clear in his tone.

"We're not thinking big enough. You won't let me pay you—"

"Non-negotiable." Ricky folded his arms, his chin set in an obstinate angle at odds with his round face. "I'm not taking money from you."

I patted the air. "Yeah, yeah. I get it. Hold on for a minute, okay?" I pulled out my phone and dialed Taryn, putting the call on speaker. "Hey, Taryn. You're on speaker with me and Ricky."

"This had better be good, Maz, or Haley's going to have your scalp. We're heading for a lunch reservation she's had for a week."

"Are you driving?"

"No. She is."

"Then listen up." I held Ricky's gaze over my phone. "If you'd had to pay somebody for the house's upkeep between when Avi died and when I moved in, how much would it have run?"

"At the going rate?"

"Let's say a generous going rate."

"Just a second. Let me crunch some numbers."

I heard her murmuring something, after which Haley called "Hi, Maz. You have precisely ten seconds before I ban you from Jae-Seong's Vietnamese coffees for a month."

I chuckled. "No need for such dire threats. All I need is a number." Taryn gave me one and I whistled. "Perfect. Thanks. Enjoy your lunch." I disconnected the call.

Ricky scowled, an expression that rarely crossed his face. In fact, the only time I'd seen it was when we were talking about Liam.

"What was that about?"

"Since you won't let me pay you, and Avi and Taryn are busting my chops about spending lawsuit proceeds, how about using that money to send Sofia to Cambridge for Liam's graduation?"

He blinked, his scowl disappearing. "You... You'd do that?"

"Absolutely. Based on the estimate Taryn gave me for a decade's worth of yard maintenance, it'll be first class all the way. Airfare, swanky hotel, car service, the whole nine." I had a check for $125,000 burning a hole in my desk at this very moment, and this could carve a very nice chunk out of it in a totally guilt-free way.

"Maz. You can't spend that much on... on..."

"On making Sofia's dream come true? Why not?" I held my hand out. When he clutched it, I brought our joined hands to my chest. "I don't want the relationship we're building to be the kind that keeps score." I'd had one of those with Greg, and one was more than enough. "Even if we never progress any farther than really good friends, I'd like to think we'd still be family."

"Yeah." He cleared his throat again. "Okay."

"Good. Then I'm taking that money and spending as much as it takes to make sure Sofia sees the results of what she's been paying for over the last four years." I smiled down at him. "The trip of a lifetime. What do you say?"

CHAPTER FIVE

Ricky's gaze cut to the door. "It's an incredibly generous offer, Maz, but she's almost seventy and a confirmed homebody. This might be too overwhelming for her to handle alone."

"Then go with her." I shrugged. "Trip of a lifetime for two."

He narrowed his eyes. "Is this your sneaky way to get me to take money I don't want?"

Well, yes, but I knew a frontal assault wouldn't work. Although I might be sneaky, I wasn't boneheaded.

"Send somebody else, then. Your sister, for instance. She's the most level-headed seventeen-year-old I've ever met."

Ricky opened his mouth, clearly about to protest, but then a contemplative expression settled onto his face. "That might work. Felicia's organized enough that she could handle logistics for an international trading company. A little trip across the country?" He scoffed. "Eso no es nada. She's also the only person other than me who can keep Tia on track with her meds."

I tapped a finger on the back of his hand, which I still held to my chest and was in no hurry to release. "You've mentioned her meds before. Would the trip be too much for her health?"

"No. She's had supraventricular tachycardia all her life, but when it started to worsen, her doctor put her on beta blockers and it's manageable."

"Is she a candidate for ablation?"

Ricky's eyebrows lifted. "You know about SVT?"

I nodded. "My grandmother had it, too. The episodes got more frequent and longer as she got older, so she finally went the surgical route." I chuckled. "She complained that if she'd known it worked so well, she'd have done it years earlier."

"Tia's still resisting the procedure because surgery makes her nervous, and as long as she keeps up with her meds and doesn't overdo, she's fine. However." He squeezed my hands. "Before you start calling airlines and booking hotel rooms, we should ask her if it's something she'd want. She's never flown before. She's never even been out of Oregon."

"What? Never?"

Ricky shrugged. "She always said there was never anywhere she wanted to go badly enough."

"You think she wants this badly enough?"

Ricky huffed a half-laugh. "Not for her. But for Liam? Yeah. Yeah, I'm pretty sure she does, but it should still be her choice."

"Then let's ask her when we ask her about the party."

"Ai." He released my hands and stepped back. "I forgot about the party. We can't do both."

I stuck my hands in my back pockets so I wouldn't reach for him again. "Why not? The party's not until June first, and she scheduled it so Liam would have time to get home for it. We'll send her a few days ahead of time. She and Felicia can see the sights, visit with Liam—"

"Assuming he can carve out time from his busy schedule for them," Ricky said dryly.

"Even if he doesn't, they can still go to the ceremony and then fly home by the thirty-first. Meanwhile, we can prep everything here for the party. All she'll have to do is hang out with her family and show everyone pictures of the trip."

Ricky closed the distance between us and looked up at me. "You'd do that for my family?"

I had to try twice before I could speak, because with Ricky's warm brown eyes on me, I'd somehow forgotten where I kept my voice. "I'd do that for *our* family. I may only have been here in Ghost for a few weeks, but I'm already home."

Ricky leaned forward, and I was *sure* he was going to kiss me this time, his gaze locked on mine. Closer. Closer. Clo—

"Enrique? Por favor, could you help me with this tray?"

His gaze snapped from my face to the porch where Sofia was standing in the doorway, a laden lacquered tray in her hands. "Tia, you didn't have to bring the whole pitcher."

"You boys looked thirsty. What was I to do?"

"Stay there. We'll drink on the steps."

The two of us climbed the gentle grassy slope. Ricky relieved Sofia of the tray and set it town on the porch at the top of the steps. He nodded at the rocking chair that was drawn up next to the railing. "You sit. I'll pour." As she settled herself on the colorful embroidered cushions, Ricky said, "Tia. Why are there only two glasses?"

She folded her hands in her lap. "I am not the one who has been working all morning."

"Nevertheless, you can join us." He turned to me, the pitcher in his hand. "Maz, would you mind grabbing another glass from the cabinet?"

"No problem."

I toed off my badly battered sneakers at the threshold—hey, I wasn't about to wear my marginally less battered Converse to garden in—and walked inside, pushing the door closed with my hip. I couldn't contaminate Sofia's pristine kitchen or open her cabinets, let alone collect a glass, with hands that had been sweating inside suede gloves for the last two hours. I'd been in Sofia's house often enough by now that the route through the living room and down the hall to the bathroom was familiar, but all the way, I mentally kicked my butt.

Had I *really* just told Ricky that I'd adopted myself into his *family*? I knew how seriously he and all his relatives took that concept, whether they were related by blood, marriage, or ceremony, like the christening that made Ricky Sofia's godson. He'd told me almost the first time we'd met that how important that commitment was to her.

But I wasn't related in any of those ways. Yes, I'd found a belonging place in Ghost, but inviting myself into Ricky's family without his consent? I mean, I *thought* we were heading in that direction, but he didn't seem to be in any rush. For that matter, I was feeling a little cautious and gun-shy myself.

As in literally, since the last guy who'd made a move on me had threatened me with a gun.

"Get over yourself, Maz," I told my reflection in the mirror over the sink as I scrubbed my hands with Sofia's honeysuckle-scented soap. "If I overstepped, I'll apologize and back off. If I didn't? Well, that would be great."

I couldn't deny that something under my heart yearned to truly be a part of this community, including the Vargas clan, the scope of which seemed to grow by the day. But I'd been here less than a month. I had time.

Time to take my time.

I owned a house here, for Pete's sake, a house that I shared with a permanent resident ghost. I planned to live here for the rest of my life, to make this town my home. Alienating anybody, let alone my next-door neighbor and a man I was seriously attracted to, would be awkward to say the least. I had enough failed relationships in my past. The last thing I needed was to start a new collection here in Ghost.

"Too bad there's not a soap that can wash away anxiety, regret, and poor decisions, because I'd be seriously tempted to break into the royalty money for something like that."

Until I could find it, though, I'd just have to deal with my own crap the best I could. So I dried my hands and returned to the kitchen to collect a tumbler from the kitchen cabinet.

When I stepped out onto the porch, Sofia was cradling her glass of tea in both hands. Ricky had returned the pitcher to the tray next to the remaining empty glass instead of serving himself, which was exactly on point with what I knew about him, even after such a short acquaintance: He always put others first.

I closed the door behind me and handed him the new glass. "Here you go."

He looked up at me from his seat on the top step, his smile bright. "Gracias." He took a deep breath, and I thought he was about to say something else, but then a gust of wind ruffled his hair and his gaze slid from mine to a spot behind me. "Maz, if you wouldn't mind, could you close the door again? Give it a good yank. The latch is sticky, and it doesn't always catch. I think I need to adjust the strike plate."

"Sure." I gave the door a good yank as directed, trying not to think about other things that might get yanked in the future if I was lucky. When I sat down and leaned against the post on the other side of the steps, Ricky was already holding out a full glass for me. "Thanks."

He poured his own last, of course. "Tia, have you thought more about your party?"

She gazed down at her untouched tea. "It is not my party. It was a party for Guillermo. There is not much point if he cannot be here."

"Why?" Ricky pulled himself up and tried to look affronted —a total fail on his perpetually cheerful face. "Are you saying the rest of us aren't worthy of a party?"

Sofia made a shooing motion. "Do not be fresh, Enrique. You know that is not the point."

"I know I'm not part of the family," I said, "but—"

"Nonsense, Maz." Sofia rocked her chair forward so she could reach my shoulder and give it a pat. "Of course you are family. You and your gatito both."

If Sofia had accepted me, that was something anyway. I'd learned enough about Ricky's extended clan to know that she was its beating heart, even though she was only a Vargas by marriage.

"If that's the case…" I glanced at Ricky and he gave a little nod, as if to say *it's your move.* "I have a proposal. How would you like to attend Lia— that is, Guillermo's graduation ceremony?"

Her snowy brows drew together. "His ceremony? How? It is all the way on the other side of the country."

"It is. But a plane can get you there in about six hours. You could go to Massachusetts, to Cambridge. Stay at a nice hotel. See the sights."

Her eyes got a faraway look. "I have always wanted to see the campus where Guillermo has spent so many happy years." She shook her head. "But it is impossible. Those airplanes, those hotels. They are expensive. And Guillermo's law school costs even more. I could not afford it."

"You wouldn't have to."

She looked from me to Ricky, clearly confused. "What do you mean?"

"I mean that Ricky took perfect care of my house—the outside of it, anyway—for ten years without taking a penny for it."

"Pfft." She batted the air. "That is nothing. This is what family does, and Avi and Oren, they were family."

"Nevertheless, he's banked some serious goodwill with me and Av— with me, so I'd like the graduation trip to be my gift to you."

Her eyes widened. "But… but I could not go alone. I do not know the city, and Guillermo will be so busy."

"Take Felicia with you. I've met her. There's nobody I've ever met who's more on board with tackling an unfamiliar city than she is."

Hope flickered across Sofia's face, but then she firmed her lips and shook her head. "No. It is too much. I cannot accept such a thing."

"But Sofia," I said, arranging my face in what I hoped was sincere hurt, "this is what family does. If you refuse, it would mean you don't think I belong in yours."

She narrowed her eyes and set her glass down on the porch with a *clunk*. "Maz Amani, you are using my own words against me."

I grinned. "Is it working?"

She threw up her hands. "You are as fresh as Enrique. There is no way I can win. If I say no, then I am denying your place. If I say yes, I am taking something worth far too much."

I took her hand. "Say yes, Sofia. You've supported your grandson all through his college years. He's about to walk across the stage and get his diploma placed in his hand. Don't you want to see that?"

Her throat worked for a moment as she swallowed twice. Tears glistened in her eyes as she whispered, "Sí. Sí, I do."

CHAPTER SIX

Once Sofia got past her initial protests, she was all in, nearly sparkling with excitement.

"Enrique, do you really think Felicia will agree to the trip? What if she were to miss her own graduation? I'm sure one of the cousins would be happy to go with me."

"Be serious, Tia. If any of the cousins challenged her for the honor, she'd... well, she wouldn't do anything *physical* to them, nor threaten the trip for you, but she'd find a way to make them regret it once they got back. Besides, her graduation isn't until mid-June and you told me Harvard's is May twenty-ninth. You'll both head to Cambridge a few days before the ceremony and return a day or two afterward, putting you home just in time for the party. Which," he said as she opened her mouth to argue, "Maz and I will arrange along with Papi and Mami, so you don't have to worry about a thing."

She scooted forward in the chair and took my face between her smooth, dry palms. "Thank you, mijo." She kissed my forehead. "I cannot tell you how much this means to me."

"You're very welcome."

"Oh! I must tell Guillermo. He will be so excited." She beckoned to Ricky. "Enrique. You have your phone. Could you call him, por favor?"

Ricky hesitated for a moment, but then dug his phone out of the back pocket of his Wranglers. "Sure, Tia." He keyed in a number and held out the phone.

"No, no. Put on the speaker so we can all hear."

We heard two rings and then the call connected. "Ricky. What do you want?"

Ricky slid a glance at me and I buried a snort at Liam's peeved tone. Sofia didn't clock it—either the glance or the tone —because she was beaming down at the screen.

"Oh, Guillermo. I have such wonderful news!"

"Sofia? I've told you, I go by Liam now."

He calls her Sofia, not abuela or even grandmother? What the hell? Ricky had told me Liam had changed his name from Guillermo to Liam and taken his stepfather's name—Frost—in his quest to be less "ethnic." But even if he couldn't manage abuela, surely he could find some way to acknowledge the relationship.

"Yes, yes. Perdóneme, but I was so excited that I forgot."

"What are you doing with Ricky's phone, anyway? Does he know you lost your last two? He won't thank you if you lose his as well."

"Enrique is here with me. I asked him to make the call."

"Afternoon, Liam." Ricky's voice was neutral, with no trace of its usual warmth. "So nice to hear your voice."

"Ah. You're on speaker."

"We are."

"Then be sure to get your phone back from Sofia. You know her record with cell phones." He laughed, and a more condescending sound I'd never heard. "You don't want yours to be her latest victim."

"I'm touched by your concern, but maybe you should listen to Tia instead. She has news for you."

"News?" Liam's voice carried a hint of... something. Maybe suspicion? I couldn't tell. It was always easier for me to figure out the nuances of people's voices once I'd actually met them in person and seen how their words interacted with their body language.

"Yes, it is so wonderful. Wait until you hear."

"Have you finally decided to sell the house, then?"

My eyebrows shot up. Sell the house? What?

But Sofia laughed, almost gaily. "Of course not. Why would I do that?"

"It's a big place, Sofia. Maybe too big for you to handle on your own. Wouldn't a smaller place be easier for you to manage now?"

"I have no trouble with my house. Not with Enrique and the rest of the family to help."

"They have other obligations, Sofia. Their own lives. You can't expect them to drop everything for you."

"Oh." Sofia glanced at her garden and then at me, clearly about to apologize for imposing on us, but Ricky stepped in.

"Don't worry about us, Liam. We're fine. Tia's fine. The house is fine. Everything is fine. Now maybe listen to her instead of jumping to conclusions."

"Listen, Ricky, you—"

"Boys, boys. There is no need to fight. Guillermo, I am coming to see you!"

"It's Lia— What?"

"I am coming for your graduation. To see you receive your diploma."

Liam cleared his throat. "Now, Sofia. We've talked about this before. The travel would be too much for you. With your heart —"

"My heart is doing much better. My new medicine takes care of it."

"I'm glad to hear that. You're sure? The last one seemed to work at first too, but it didn't last."

"It is fine." Sofia was starting to sound uncertain.

"You should think about this seriously, Sofia. Between the ceremony itself, moving to new lodgings, and starting the internship, I won't have a minute to spare. You'll be alone in a strange city. Why go to the trouble, stress, and expense of traveling all the way across the country just to sit in a hotel by yourself?"

"I know you will be busy, and I do not expect you to babysit me. But you should have someone from your family there to see you graduate. You've worked so hard for this."

"That's true, but—"

"It is so like you to worry about me, but you needn't. I won't be alone. Felicia will be with me."

"Felicia?" Liam's tone sharpened. "You're paying Felicia's airfare? Can you afford it? I know my tuition makes it tough for you, and I promise I'll make it all up to you once I'm practicing law, but—"

"I am not paying for anything. This is a gift from my wonderful neighbor." She winked at me, chuckling. "Although I think it is more in honor of Enrique and the good care he took of the house for all these years."

"Sofia." I couldn't mistake the rebuke in Liam's tone. "You can't impose on a stranger like that."

Ricky looked as though the top of his head was about to blow off as the joy in Sofia's face was replaced by uncertainty, and I'd had enough.

"Hey, Liam. I'm Maz Amani, your abuela's new neighbor, and I can assure you it's my pleasure and privilege to gift Sofia with the trip. She's very proud of you, you know. Talks about you all the time."

"I... see. Well, I appreciate you stepping in when the rest of the family couldn't."

"Look, Liam." Yep, no doubt about it. Ricky was about to combust. "If you—"

"I'm sure the rest of the family would have stepped up, no problem, but I got there first, and I insisted. Sofia and Felicia will be arriving a few days before the ceremony so they can sightsee for a bit. Do you think you might be able to carve out a little time to have lunch or dinner with them? Despite how busy you'll be, you'll still need to eat."

Liam laughed, although it sounded forced. "Yes. Certainly. And I don't mean to sound ungrateful."

In a pig's eye, as Ricky was fond of saying. "Of course not."

"Sofia, I'll speak with you later about this. In the meantime, I really must go. I have finals to prepare for."

"Adios, Guillermo. I love you, mijo."

"Goodbye."

Ricky tucked his phone away. "I didn't realize you'd lost your phone, Tia. I'll pick up a new one for you this afternoon."

She waved his words away and stood. "I am in no hurry. I may still find the others. They must be around here somewhere, or perhaps at the restaurant. I go to so few other places."

I collected all the tea glasses and set them on the tray next to the pitcher. When I rose, Sofia immediately embraced me.

"Gracias, Maz. You have made Guillermo and me so very happy." She winked at Ricky. "And I imagine Felicia will be happy, too. I must go inside to call her on the kitchen phone and let her know." She motioned for Ricky to hand her the tray.

He shook his head. "I'll take it inside for you."

"Do not be silly. If you get the door for me, I can manage for myself. I am sure you boys have many other things to do today." She kissed his cheek and then mine. "Gracias for planting my garden."

Ricky relented, handed her the tray, and made sure to, er, yank the door after she went inside.

"So." I tucked my thumbs through my belt loops as we left Sofia's porch and ambled toward my house. "Was it my imagination, or did ol' Liam seem less than enthused? You'd think he'd be happy that someone from his family would be there to see him graduate."

Ricky snorted. "I expect he doesn't want his fancy Ivy League friends to know about his less than fancy—and less white—family. He's spent most of his life pretending we don't exist."

"Except when he's taking Sofia's money. What's the deal with her cell phones?" I knew she'd had one when we first met. She'd used it to call Ricky to clear sawdust out of my door locks.

"She's misplaced a couple. She doesn't walk around with them glued to her hand like Felicia does, or always in a pocket or purse. She's right in that she doesn't go to many places anymore. She's still got her driver's license, and she's got a car. A 2012 Corolla that belonged to my uncle Ramon, her second husband. But she doesn't drive it. Hasn't for years."

I took a left to walk between the houses and Ricky followed me around to my front yard. "Does it still run?"

He nodded as we mounted the porch steps. "I make sure of it. She lets Felicia use it, too, but most of the time it sits in her garage."

I squinted at Sofia's house. "She has a garage?"

"It's detached. The drive opens onto Birch Street." He pointed toward the road that dead-ended at the Manor grounds, perpendicular to my street, Iris Lane. "Did you notice the building beyond the garden?"

"Um... Not really?" I'd been paying more attention to Ricky's butt as he'd bent over the plants. From the quirk of his eyebrow and the tilt of his lips, I figured he was onto me. "I hope you're not going to bust my chops about that, too. Everybody's on my case today. If it's not Taryn and you about my car, it's Avi about my clothes and my stuff."

"Stuff? What stuff?"

"A bunch of boxes that are still tucked in the back of my ex's closet." I frowned as we mounted the front porch steps, picturing the stack of battered cardboard. "Although now that I think of it, he made me shift everything up to the attic when I moved out."

Ricky's eyes narrowed. "You still have things at your old boyfriend's house?"

"Yeah. Not a lot, but the boxes were bulky and wouldn't fit in the Civic when Gil and I first drove down here."

"That is not acceptable."

I paused with my hand on the doorknob. "Is this about the car again? Because I doubt the Civic would make the two round trips necessary to haul everything back here."

"No." His grin held an unfamiliar edge, and it sent a zing from my nape to my heel. "*This* is your home now, and you should have all your treasures around you."

"You sound like Avi. And I'm not sure most of my stuff would count as treasures."

The edge sharpened. "Also, you should have no more reasons to speak to that cabrón ever again. Lucky for you"—he gestured to the curb—"you have a friend with a pickup. It's barely noon and only a three-hour drive to Portland. Let's go."

"Uh. Wow. Okay. Thanks." I wiped my hands on my jeans, which only succeeded in transferring residual garden dirt to my palms. To be done with Greg for good? Yes, please. However… "Could we postpone the trip until tomorrow?" I needed time to gird my mental loins for the confrontation—and probably should give Greg a heads-up that I'd be showing up at his door.

"Tomorrow, then." He backed up until he was at the top of the steps. "I'll pick you up at eight."

Before I could do anything more than nod, he was off the porch and across the lawn.

CHAPTER SEVEN

"Ready for this?" Ricky asked.

I peered through his windshield at Greg's building, a converted warehouse in Portland's Pearl District. "Not sure I'd ever be truly ready."

"Hey." Ricky unbuckled his seatbelt and turned to face me. "I pretty much strong-armed you into this trip. If you'd rather not deal with it, we can just go home again."

Home. Home is good.

"No." I managed a smile. "Let's not. I'm a master at procrastination and conflict avoidance, so I'd have found excuses to put this off forever. And despite my griping about Greg's inhospitality, I really shouldn't impose on him any longer." My smile turned more sincere. I hoped. "Thanks for the push. I needed it." It was beyond time to tie up this loose end and get on with my new life.

Which, hopefully, would continue to include Ricky.

We climbed out of the truck, and when he joined me by the passenger door, I said, "I'm going to owe you lunch at least after this. Maybe dinner too."

He grinned at me and patted the shell that covered the truck bed. It hadn't been there yesterday, so he'd installed it just for this trip.

Just for me.

"I won't say no to either of those. Your stuff will be safe, even if we have to park for a while."

I swallowed and made myself take the first step forward. "His condo is on the top floor. I called yesterday to let him know we were coming."

"Did he answer?"

"Voicemail."

We hadn't actually spoken since I'd moved out. His response to my texts was always the same: *No messages, no mail, screw you.* Come to think of it, I hadn't texted him lately either, not since I'd moved to Ghost.

"Guess we'll see if A) he's home, B) he'll open the door for us, and C) he didn't actually dump all my stuff on the curb months ago."

Ricky's black brows drew together. "Do you think he'd do something like that?"

I led the way inside to the elevator lobby. "Nah. That'd mean he'd have to move those boxes by himself. He wouldn't exert himself that much and he definitely wouldn't have paid anybody else to do it."

"Then I guess we'll find out." He gestured to the intercom. "I'd ring it for you, but I think it would be better for you to do the honors." He grinned. "Closure, and all that."

I choked back a laugh as I pressed the buzzer. "You have a point."

A moment later, Greg's voice emerged from the speaker. "Yes?"

"It's Maz."

"Maz." His tone was perfectly flat.

"Greg." I matched it. Also perfectly.

"This isn't a good time."

"I called yesterday. If you wanted to reschedule, you should have replied to my message."

His long-suffering sigh was audible—and drawn out far longer than necessary. "Fine. Come up."

The elevator doors slid open. Ricky gestured me inside. "After you."

When we stepped out of the car, Greg was standing in his open door in his standard weekend casual chinos and polo shirt.

"This is super inconvenient, Maz. I do have things to do, you know."

"It's half a dozen boxes, Greg. It'll take us twenty minutes to move them out and then you can stop complaining about them taking up your valuable attic space. BT-dub, if you hadn't blown off the lawyer who was looking for me by telling her I was dead, I'd have removed them three months ago."

He crossed his arms. "And put them where, exactly?"

I can admit it—I smirked. "In my new house, exactly."

Greg snorted. "Like you can afford a house. You can't even maintain your car."

"That car's history, anyway," Ricky said. "He's getting a new one."

Greg's jaw sagged. "Wait. What?"

"Hey." I poked Ricky's biceps, which were his best feature. Other than his smile. And his eyes. And his hair. And his butt. Not to mention his heart. "I haven't agreed to that yet."

Ricky's smile was decidedly smug. "You will."

"Brother," I muttered. "Everybody needs to get off my case about the car." I pushed my curls off my forehead. "Greg, this is Ricky Vargas. Ricky, Greg Findler."

Greg's left foot in its Bruno Magli loafer began to tap in a cadence I knew all too well: his you're-wasting-my-time-but-I'm-keeping-my-annoyance-in-check tempo. It was a little slower than his if-you-don't-do-what-I-want-I'll-bring-out-my-killer-passive-aggressiveness beat and a little faster than his get-to-the-point-because-I've-got-better-things-to-do roll.

Greg's toe taps had a vocabulary all their own.

"I suppose," he drawled, "that once more you've conned someone into believing you'll actually return a favor." He turned his head in Ricky's direction, but his gaze was focused on the wall behind us. "I should warn you. He'll never make good on it."

Ricky never lost his affable expression. "In my family, we don't keep score that way. But if we did, Maz would have banked about a decade's worth of credit when he decided to send my godmother and sister to Boston for my cousin's graduation."

Greg's chiseled jaw sagged. "He what? How?" He turned a glare on me. "If you've got money, you owe me."

"Owe you for what?"

"For storing your boxes."

I sighed. He did have a point. "Was it difficult to move them out of the way for your own things?"

"Not exactly." His gaze slid away from mine. "The area isn't easily accessible."

"Yeah, because it's an *attic*. Its purpose is to keep stuff out of the way." I narrowed my eyes. "You badgered the reno company for weeks so they'd lower the bedroom ceilings and create that space. Have you put *anything* up there at all?"

"No," he mumbled.

"Are you *planning* to put anything up there? Ever?"

His nostrils flared. "You know that's not the point."

"Look, Greg. When I lived here, I paid my share. I offered to put everything in a storage locker, but you said as long as I moved everything to the attic myself—which I did—that I could leave it there until I found a new place. Well, I've found a new place and I've come to get everything out of your hair. We can finally be done."

Ricky cocked his head. "You know something? I think that's why he agreed to keep it, Maz. He doesn't *want* to be done."

"This is none of your business," Greg said hotly.

"Maybe it wasn't before. But it is now. Are you going to let us in?"

For a minute, I gaped at Ricky. "What?" I croaked.

"Think about it, Maz. He always responded to your texts, even if he was a jerk about it. If he truly wanted to ghost you, he would have maintained radio silence. Not to mention he pointedly did *not* tell you not to come by today after you left that message."

I glanced at Greg's reddening face. "I'm pretty sure he—"

"Also, that much cologne should be illegal."

Greg flung the door open. "Get the damn boxes already. Don't mar the walls, and if you scatter any dust or trash around, you're cleaning it up."

"I always did, Greg. I always did."

I led the way through the sunny great room. Regardless of how my relationship with Greg had ended, I'd always appreciated the design and execution of the space, although industrial chic had never been my vibe. I much preferred my Queen Anne beauty in Ghost.

The small second bedroom where I'd worked was at the end of a short hallway, the desk still under the wide window. The center of the room was clear, so I pointed to the trap in the ceiling.

"Stairs to the attic."

"Good." Ricky glanced over his shoulder to where Greg loomed in the doorway. "'Cause I doubt he'd loan us a ladder."

"He'd have to buy one first."

The hook I'd used to open the trap was standing in the corner, exactly where I'd left it months ago. With it in my hands, it only took a few seconds to snag the recessed handle overhead and pull—I'd had practice, after all. The stairs extended smoothly, although dust motes danced in the sunlight. I offered up a brief thank-you to Avi, who kept our house completely dust free.

I mounted the steps until I could see over the attic floor. My boxes still sat exactly where I'd left them, as far as I could tell. I went the rest of the way up the stairs.

When Ricky joined me a minute later, I was standing with my hand on the top box.

"Is this everything?"

"Y-yes." I rubbed my chest, easing a sudden pang. "I didn't remember there being so many. I thought there were only six."

These boxes held everything that was left from my childhood, from my life with my parents, from their lives. When their RV went off the road in the Rockies, everything they'd had with them had been lost, too. Even ten boxes weren't a lot to show for three lives.

Ricky sidled up next to me until his shoulder bumped mine. "You okay?"

"I will be." I patted the top box. "This one has all my dad's kitchen stuff that he didn't take with him when he and Mom embraced van life. He kept his recipes in a few loose-leaf notebooks." I glanced at Ricky. "Did I ever tell you that my grandfather on Dad's side was the youngest of thirteen? My grandmother was the youngest of seven."

Ricky's eyebrows shot up. "You must have tons of cousins, too."

"Maybe. But not all of them emigrated to the US, and they were mostly all a generation older than me. My mom and dad were both only children, so no first cousins for me, and my mom never introduced me to any of her extended family." Which was why I'd never known about Oren.

He squeezed my arm. "You've got another family now."

I swiped a hand under my eyes. "Yeah. I do." I took a deep breath. "Anyway, Dad's cookbooks have handwritten recipes for his aunt's pita bread, his dad's cheese, my grandmother's kibbe. I haven't seen them for almost a year. Haven't cooked any of them for even longer."

"Why not?"

"Greg doesn't care for Arabic food, and he had nothing but scorn for my mom's recipes." I chuckled softly. "Not that there are many of those. Mom hated to cook. She said it was the principle of the thing—in her midwestern fundamentalist family, cooking and cleaning were always the women's responsibility, and she refused to bow to the patriarchy. But I think she just found cooking so boring that she didn't see the point when she could grab a bowl of cereal and spend her time reading instead."

Ricky studied where my hand rested on the box. "Will you make some of your dad's dishes for me?"

The pang in my chest eased for the first time since I'd come into the attic. "If you'd like me to, sure. Although I confess to being a little intimidated. I'm not the fantastic cook my dad was, and your family runs a restaurant with the best Mexican food I've eaten anywhere except Sofia's kitchen. I doubt I can measure up to your standards."

He shrugged. "Sometimes it's the willingness to give the gift that matters more than the gift itself."

"All right," I murmured. "It's a date."

"Hey!" Greg called. "I do have other places to be today."

Trust Greg to kill the mood.

Ricky pointed to the stairs. "Pass me the boxes and I'll stack them in the room below."

Once we'd done that, we carted them out with a hand truck Ricky had produced from somewhere. As we wheeled out of the condo on the third and last trip, Greg closed the door behind me for the final time.

"Twenty minutes on the nose." Ricky poked the elevator button. "You called it."

When the doors slid open and we stepped inside, I could have sworn that I floated an inch off the floor like Avi often did. I'd been buried under the shambles of this relationship for so long, had gotten so used to living in its ruins, that I hadn't realized how much it had been weighing me down.

My steps as we walked to Ricky's truck and loaded the boxes in the back were lighter than they'd been in over a year.

Ricky closed the tailgate and locked the shell hatch. "Ready to head home?"

"Not yet." I grinned at him. "I promised you lunch, remember? And I know just the place."

CHAPTER EIGHT

"That was fantastic." Ricky dropped his crumpled napkin into the plastic basket that had held his sandwich and grinned at me across the table. "I've never had falafel before."

I took the last swig of my water. "It was one of my dad's favorite foods."

"Did he cook it often?"

"Almost never, and when he did, it was just cooking frozen patties he bought at the local Middle Eastern market because he could never get a texture that he liked when he made it from scratch." I stood and stacked our baskets while Ricky collected our empty water bottles. "He was always on the lookout for restaurants that served it, looking for the best option."

We deposited our trash and recyclables in the bins by the door and waited while a group of women in workout gear entered before stepping outside.

"He ever find any?" Ricky asked.

"Occasionally, yes, but he had very high standards." I backed up to the middle of the sidewalk, the better to see the sign above the restaurant's window. "He loved this place. My grandmother lived here when I was a kid and we used to come here whenever we visited her."

"You miss them." Ricky moved closer, also gazing upward as though he didn't want to invade my privacy by forcing eye contact.

My throat was tight enough that I couldn't answer, so I just nodded.

"Do you miss this?" He gestured to the street. "The city, things like this restaurant?" The streetcar dinged behind us as it whirred smoothly along its tracks, and he smiled crookedly. "Public transportation as an alternative to your patético car?"

"My car is not pathetic." However, my knee-jerk retort was, because my voice broke like a thirteen-year-old's.

Someone passed us and walked into the restaurant, sending the bell over its door tinkling, and I was hit by a sudden longing for Isaksen's. For my front porch. For the rolling expanse of the Manor grounds across my quiet street.

For Ghost.

"You know something? I don't think I do." I took a deep, steadying breath, the old chains of grief losing another link or two. "As much as I love Portland, I've found something I love even more."

I turned my head to smile at him and caught my breath because his warm brown cheek was *this close* to my lips. Then Ricky turned his head slightly so *his* lips were *this close* to mine...

And then the door to a glassed-in vestibule next to the restaurant flew open, and a young guy with a *very* big dog on a *very* flimsy leash bounded out onto the sidewalk. The guy flashed us a smile before he turned toward the corner, but the dog dropped his hindquarters and skidded to a stop, his toenails scraping the concrete. He skittered in a circle and lunged straight at me, and yep, that leash was just as flimsy as I'd thought, because it didn't restrain him in the least.

Suddenly, the dog's square white muzzle was inches from my belly, and I was staring into a pair of practically glowing yellow eyes.

"Good doggie," I croaked.

The dog's nose quivered, and he began lowering his head when the guy barked, "Doop! No butt sniffing!"

The dog backed off, his red ears flattening, as the guy strode over and grabbed his collar. "I'm so sorry. He's usually better behaved on the street, but some lessons are harder to teach, you know?"

"No worries." I brushed at my jeans. "He probably just smelled my cat."

"Oh." The guy's sunny smile grew. "I never thought of that. Maybe he wasn't backsliding after all." He gazed down at the dog with clear affection, the leash once more in evidence. "Sorry if I misjudged you, boy." He lifted a hand to us. "Have a nice day. C'mon, Doop."

As they loped off down the street, I glanced at Ricky and looked away when I saw that *he* was glancing at me. I mentally rolled my eyes. We were both thirty-year-old gay men, and we were acting like preteens with a first crush.

But I didn't want to rush things. What was growing between us was already important and might turn into *essential*. I didn't want to jeopardize that by pushing for anything that he wasn't ready for. Heck, that *I* wasn't ready for, considering that the rubble of my last lapse in relationship judgment was presently loaded in his truck.

I winced internally. Yeah, maybe bringing Ricky face to face with Greg wasn't the best way to move our own relationship forward. Maybe I should send the guy and his dog a thank-you note and a really big dog biscuit for interrupting what could have been a giant misstep.

"So. Um." My gaze caught on the window of a shop on the other side of the vestibule. "Oh, hey. Crystals." I pointed at the display that included jewelry as well as loose stones. "Maybe there's something in there that Patrice could use in her shop. Do you mind if we step inside for a minute before we head home?"

Ricky blinked twice and shook his head slightly, as though he were coming up from being underwater. I wasn't sure if his smile held a rueful edge or not. "I don't think she's looking to increase her inventory. The store doesn't get much traffic. But I'm in no hurry."

"Great. Um. Yeah. Great."

When we walked in, we were greeted by the scent of sandalwood with undertones of vanilla, along with the sound of water burbling over stones from an indoor fountain. A woman wearing multiple layers of trailing gauze in graduated shades of purple was weaving a willow branch into a wreath.

Smiling, she set the wreath aside and lifted her hand. I nearly returned the Vulcan live long and prosper salute before I realized her gesture was something completely different.

"Blessed be," she said, her sleeve fluttering way too close to the row of lit candles on the counter behind her.

"Hi." I charged toward her, right hand thrust forward. Not the most graceful of greetings, perhaps, but I really wanted her to lower her arm.

Hey, I ghostwrote a series of fire safety pamphlets for a risk management company, and those examples really stick with you, know what I'm saying?

To give her due credit, she graciously shook my hand. "I'm Lenore. May I help you find what you seek?"

"Not really seeking anything. A friend of ours has a similar shop back in our hometown and…" Yeesh. Way to make it more awkward by suggesting we might be scoping the place out for a competitor.

However, she clasped her hands, and I recognized the expression on her face because I'd seen it on people at countless fan-based conventions when they discovered another member of their tribe.

"We're always pleased to find other practitioners. Do you have one of their business cards?"

I had never even been inside Patrice's shop, which made me wince. I should rectify that sooner rather than later. "No, I—"

"Sure." Ricky pulled out his wallet, extracted a card from an inner pocket, and handed it to Lenore. "The owner's name is Patrice DeHaven, but this is the manager's card."

Lenore took it, running her finger over the embossed text. "Strings and Stones. Intriguing. Thank you. I shall certainly give them a call." She looked up and winked at Ricky. "And perhaps ask for knitting pattern recommendations."

We left her to her wreath and strolled around the store. When I was checking out the book selection, I heard Ricky chuckle behind me. When I turned, he had his cell phone in his hand.

He caught my gaze and held it up. On the screen was a photo, clearly taken with a selfie stick, of Felicia and Sofia standing in front of Nordstrom Rack. "Felicia took Tia to Eugene to shop for the trip." He looked down at the screen. "I suspect that they're at the Rack more for Felicia, though. It doesn't seem much like Tia's style."

"You never know," I said as we left the shop with a wave at Lenore. "Maybe she'll find a new vibe now that she'll be a continental traveler." Something caught my eye from inside the vestibule. "Hold on a sec, please?"

"Sure." He tucked his hands in the pockets of his denim jacket and stepped aside so he wasn't blocking the sidewalk.

I peered through the glass door, shading my eyes against the glare. A flyer featuring the graphic of a cartoon ghost was tacked on a bulletin board opposite a bank of mailboxes.

When I was living in Portland, I must have passed this place a hundred times, but I'd never noticed that flyer before. Granted, I'd had no reason to look inside the vestibule—in fact, I don't remember ever seeing it, and the flyer might be a new addition. But even so, I doubt that it would have caught my eye if it weren't for Avi.

Product identification. That's what my college marketing teacher called it. I only noticed things related to ghosts because, well, I was now related to a ghost, even if only by proximity.

The flyer advertised a company that sold ghost hunting equipment. I wasn't sure why they thought this was a good place to post their flyer, since the only foot traffic with a clear view would be the people who lived and worked in the building. Maybe it was a thumb-your-nose gesture to Lenore's occult shop?

I made a note of their website, anyway. Who knew? Maybe they'd have something that could assist with my project at the Manor.

After I stepped outside, we headed straight back to Ricky's truck. I studied his profile as he effortlessly navigated his way out of town. "Do you come to Portland often?"

He shrugged. "Now and then. One of my cousins lives up here and her kids go to high school in the district. Her daughter's on the dance team at Lincoln." He cut me a glance as he turned onto the highway. "Trust me, you haven't lived until you've spent all day on gym bleachers watching a competition. It took my butt a week to recover."

"A tragedy," I murmured.

"What was that?"

"Nothing." I watched the flow of traffic for a while before clearing my throat. "Thank you."

He didn't answer until he'd finished changing lanes. "For what?"

"For making this round trip with me. Six hours on the road, interrupted only by Greg's debatable hospitality, isn't the pleasantest way to spend your day off." I let my voice drift up a bit at the end of the sentence, hoping that Ricky might volunteer something about his actual job. However, either he didn't notice my unsubtle hint, or he chose to ignore it.

"De nada." He glanced at me and gave me a wink. "Besides, I got lunch out of the deal."

I let the matter drop. I'd learned in the few weeks of our acquaintance that Ricky was like me in that both of us appreciated quiet, especially after a meal, so we drove for a while in silence before I brandished my phone.

"I want to check out the website from that flyer, if that's okay."

"Sure. What's the company? I didn't get a good look at the ad."

"A paranormal investigation supply. They sell ghost hunting equipment."

His eyebrows rose. "Isn't that kind of redundant for you? It's not like you need to hunt a ghost. You've already found one."

"Technically, he found me first. But I'm curious. How do people who do this seriously approach the problem?" I snorted. "Thaddeus Richdale certainly never cracked that particular code."

"I guess it won't hurt to check them out."

"Nope." The home page had a helpful list of basic equipment, so I scrolled through, clicking on links that sounded interesting.

After reading the description of a device called an EVP portal, I asked, "Did anybody in Ghost ever use traditional ghost hunting gear?"

He nodded. "Several times over the years. Saul's covered the entire Manor more than once since he took over as director. No luck. Now and then, Professor DeHaven gets contacted by other so-called 'professional' ghost hunters. They sign up for her extension classes and then try to argue with her. They don't last long."

I tapped my screen with a fingernail. "Some of this equipment is for recording sounds."

"They tried that at the Manor too. Never got anything but static."

"But Peg—Marguerite Windflower, the psychic counselor I spoke to—said that something in the Manor actually repelled ghosts. If they weren't looking in a place where a ghost actually *was*, they wouldn't have gotten any results."

"That's... a good point." He flashed me a grin. "But you know exactly where a ghost is. You want to use it as proof that the equipment either works or doesn't? Beat the ghost hunters at their own game?"

"No. Not really. The last thing I need is a bunch of these guys"—I tapped my screen—"showing up on my doorstep to use Avi's presence to bolster their own reputations. I've got nothing to prove to them."

"For Saul and Patrice then?"

I shook my head. "Not for them either. I'm pretty sure they have no doubts." I glanced down at a page featuring a piece of equipment that promised voice-to-text from sounds detected along multiple radio frequencies. "For Avi."

"Avi? Surely he doesn't need proof, either."

"No, but I think he's lonely, Ricky. He's stuck there in that house, and while the house is great, he probably knows every crack and crevice by now. I'm the only one he can communicate with other than Gil, and Gil's vocabulary leaves much to be desired. But if there was a way for others to hear his voice, to have conversations with him?"

"You're right." Ricky made a sound low in his throat that provoked a completely different response in me than he probably intended. "That would mean something to him."

"So you think I should order some of this stuff?"

"Can't hurt to try."

Well, it could hurt a lot if I raised Avi's hopes and the equipment turned out to be a bunch of bogus junk. But as I've said, when it came to Avi's afterlife, we were still in the discovery process, and I was pretty sure he wouldn't blame me if the results were disappointing.

I poked around on the site a little more, added the text-to-speech tool and the EVP portal to my cart, as well as a couple of faraday bags to protect the electronics from Avi's electrical field. The total at checkout made me wince, but hey, I had a hundred and twenty-five grand sitting at home, and Sofia's trip would hardly make a dent in it.

I opted for expedited shipping at a premium, because the look in Avi's eyes when Ricky and I had left for our gardening adventure was still with me. The sooner we had a solution, the better.

Then I set my phone aside and focused on flirting with Ricky for the rest of the ride.

It was almost five when we pulled into Ghost and I sighed with contentment. "Home at last, and this time the journey was much more pleasant since it wasn't accompanied by Gil yowling in protest all the way from Portland."

Ricky chuckled. "I'm glad I rate higher than Gil as a conversationalist, then."

I smirked at him as he turned onto Iris Lane. "You have your moments."

He slowed as we approached my house and pulled up to the curb, although he didn't turn off the engine. "It'll make it easier for us to unload if you move your sorry excuse for a car so I can back the truck in."

"Careful." I stuck my nose in the air. "Keep up the insults and it might refuse to share its cozy garage."

His laughter followed me when I hopped out of the truck. We played car lotto for a few minutes—I moved my car to the street so Ricky could back up the drive and into the garage. I was delayed getting back to the truck because my driver's side door decided to resist closing more than usual.

"Stop that," I muttered as I braced my feet and shoved. "You're making us look bad."

With a last *screech-groan* of protest, the door slammed shut.

And the wheel center cap promptly fell off.

I glanced around furtively, and since I wasn't about to try opening the door again, I kicked it into the gutter to worry about later. Splaying my palm on the windshield, I whispered, "I won't tell if you don't."

CHAPTER NINE

"You're really good at this," I puffed as I hauled the last box, which seemed to contain bricks, up the stairs to my bedroom.

Ricky wasn't even breathing hard. He swung his box off his shoulder and thumped it down just inside the bedroom door. "I've had lots of practice carting things up and down these stairs. Tia's too." He flashed me a grin. "Let's just say I've never needed to hit a StairMaster."

I set my box down with a relieved huff and straightened, pressing my hands to my lower back. "In case I haven't mentioned it before? I really appreciate your help."

His gaze locked with mine. "It's my pleasure."

It suddenly struck me that we were in *my bedroom*. And that *my bed* was *right there*. I took a step forward. Ricky matched me. But before we moved any closer, there was a *chink-chink-chink* from the stairs, followed by the thud of furry paws galloping down from the attic.

An orange blur flashed by the door and I heard the telltale skitter of Gil batting something along the hardwood floor.

I raised my palms. "I'd better go see what he's stolen from poor Avi."

Ricky gestured to the door. "After you."

Just as I stepped out of the room, I heard a distant bright *clink*. Gil was standing with his head poked through the balusters, staring down into the entryway.

"Lost it already, big guy?" I ran my fingers down Gil's spine as I passed him. "I really hope you didn't break anything irreplaceable, or Avi won't be friends with you anymore."

Although considering Avi's short list of available friends, I suspected he'd cut Gil considerable slack.

"Trouble?" Ricky asked, appearing by my side.

"Gil being Gil. Just need to assess for any necessary damage control." I peered over the railing. I didn't see anything obvious, and Avi hadn't made an outraged appearance with attendant flying paper, so I trotted down the stairs, with Gil dashing along at my side.

He, of course, made a fast break at the foot of the stairs, darting in front of my feet and making me clutch at the banister to keep from taking a header onto the floor. Ricky gripped my other arm.

"Steady, there."

I met his gaze. I wasn't sure I *could* be steady with him touching me, but I managed to croak, "Thanks." Then he released me. *Dammit.* "I, um, better go see what he's got."

While we'd paused on the stairs, Gil had already chased his treasure out of the vestibule and into the family room. His head was under the sofa, his butt in the air, and his tail waving. I hauled him out.

"That'll be enough from you, Mister Sir." I held him out to Ricky. "Could you contain him for a couple of minutes while I conduct some reconnaissance?"

"No problem. Come here, gatito." Ricky scooped Gil into his arms and flipped him upside down. Gil didn't struggle in Ricky's grasp—understandable, since I wouldn't either—but he craned his neck to peer down at the floor, pupils blown into perfect black circles.

I engaged my phone's flashlight function and knelt down, sweeping the beam from one end of the sofa to the other. Nothing, not even a dust bunny, *thank you, Avi.* I'd think Gil was chasing air again—he'd been known to do that—or a random fly or moth, except air and insects didn't *chink* coming down the stairs.

I made another sweep, and I saw it: a glint of gold half-hidden by the sofa foot, and my stomach swooped, because I recognized the curve of burnished metal.

Oren's wedding band.

Dammit, Gil, this is not *something you can steal.* Avi would forgive a lot of things, but losing Oren's ring was high on the list of *not ever, not nohow.* How had he missed Gil's attack?

Oh. He must be… elsewhere.

We needed some way for us to communicate when he was in that place, wherever it was. Maybe the ghost hunting site ran to multidimensional cell phones or phantasmagorical telegraphs. I'd have to check it out, although not until the present crisis was averted.

I reached under the sofa and snagged the ring with the tip of my forefinger, drawing it across the floor until I could grab it and fold my fist around it.

When I stood, I gave Gil a stern glare, which had about as much effect as you might expect. That is to say, none. He'd stopped doing his freaky owl impression and was lying, seemingly content, in Ricky's arms, all four feet curled up to his furry belly.

I lowered my head until I was nose-to-nose with Gil. "Do I need to restrict your attic access?"

"He steal something he shouldn't?"

"You could say that." I stood and uncurled my fingers slightly so Ricky could glimpse what rested in my palm.

Ricky grimaced. "Dios."

"Exactly." I glared at Gil again. "We need to have a serious discussion about your addiction to shiny things. Maybe I should check online for gold lamé catnip mice."

"If you can't find one, I expect Tia could make one for you. She used to make toys for Princesa all the time."

"I'll have to—"

"Maz!" Avi was suddenly *right there*, occupying the space between Ricky and me. His transparent elbow must have collided with Gil and Ricky, because Gil's belly fur stood on end and Ricky startled, uttering a soft curse.

"It's all right, Avi." I held my hand up and waggled my fist. "I caught him before—"

"It's Sofia."

I took a step back. "What?"

Avi glitched, something he hadn't done since my first days in the house, when he'd still been confused and angry. "Sofia. In her garden. I saw it from the attic window." He disappeared.

"I felt *something*." Ricky set Gil down and rubbed his arm. "Was that… was that Avi?"

"Yes, but he's gone now. He said something about Sofia."

Ricky's jaw tightened. "I need to go." He strode toward the front door—and right through Avi, who'd blinked into sight again.

Both of them shuddered.

"Not that way." Avi wrung his hands. "The garden. Hurry! She collapsed."

"Avi said she collapsed in the garden. The back door is quicker."

Ricky didn't hesitate. He barreled past me and charged through the kitchen before I could take a step. From the sound of it, he'd wrenched the back door open so hard it banged against the wall. I couldn't blame him. If something was wrong with Sofia…

"We'll check it out," I assured Avi.

He ran his hands down his pants and I wondered briefly whether ghosts' palms could sweat. "Update me as soon as you know something?"

"Absolutely."

As I hurried into the kitchen, I glanced down at my hand. I didn't want to leave Oren's ring where Gil could get to it, but— "Gil!" I shoved the ring deep in my front pocket just in time to grab Gil up before he could dash past me and out the open mudroom door.

"You've caused enough trouble without me having to chase you through the neighborhood. Stay here with Avi." I set Gil in the butler's pantry and closed its swinging door. I met Avi's gaze. "I'll be back as soon as I can."

Avi nodded. "Hurry."

I stepped onto the porch and closed the door behind me. The westering sun had dipped below the stand of fir trees in Patrice's yard and cast their long shadows across my lawn. The shadows pointed directly to Ricky, kneeling next to an ominously still figure that lay in the dirt we'd turned… was it only yesterday?

I raced down the steps and across my lawn and dropped down next to him. Sofia was lying on her side, one arm extended toward a tomato plant and the other limp against her stomach. Ricky held his phone in one hand as he gently laid the fingers of his other hand against her neck.

"Is she breathing?" I asked.

"Yes, but her pulse is racing."

"An SVT episode?"

"Maybe. Maybe not." He thumbed his phone and handed it to me. "Put this on speaker, please?"

I did as he asked, laid the phone on my palm, and raised it near his face.

"9-1-1. What is your emergency?"

"My aunt has collapsed. We need an ambulance." Ricky gave them Sofia's address. "We're in the backyard. In her garden. She's breathing, but has an extremely rapid pulse."

"Help is on the way. Please stay on the line with me until they arrive. Is there anything the responders should know?"

"Yes. She has chronic SVT, but she's on beta blockers to control the condition."

"Any other medications?"

"Yes. Simvastatin, a calcium supplement, and a multivitamin."

"If you could have those available for the EMTs, that would be helpful."

Ricky looked up at me. "I hate to ask, but—"

"Just tell me where to look."

"Upstairs medicine chest. The bottles will be there along with the pill minder for the week. Bring it all?"

"You got it."

I set Ricky's phone on the ground next to him and ran up the slope to Sofia's porch. The back door was closed but not locked, so I hurried inside. I raced up the stairs to a wide landing. The sinking sun shone through a window at the end of a short hallway to my right, in the direction of my house, laying a swath of orange-yellow along the floor like a second carpet. The window to my left was already twilight-dark, shadows gathering in the corners beneath it.

A door immediately ahead of me led to a bathroom, but when I checked the medicine chest, it held only hand lotion, a bottle of witch hazel, and an unopened box of toothpaste.

Holding my hand up to shade my eyes, I found two doors at either side of the hall. One led to a spacious, airy room that didn't look like Sofia's style in the least, all leather and navy and brass. I didn't bother checking the ensuite, because this was clearly Liam's space, lovingly maintained despite him never showing up.

A smaller room across the hall was done up in vibrant reds and yellows I associated with Sofia, but it didn't have her signature honeysuckle scent, nor did it have an attached bath.

With the sun at my back, I followed my shadow across the landing again and hit pay dirt, although I had to blink for a few seconds as my vision adjusted to the dimness. In terms of size and floor plan, the room was Liam's man-suite in reverse, but the embroidered coverlet on the bed matched the throw pillows in Sofia's living room, and the rocking chair next to the window was the twin of the one on the back porch.

A half-open door next to the carved headboard revealed a glimpse of gleaming white porcelain. *Aha! Target acquired.* Movement caught my eye as I hurried across the room, making me stumble for a moment. However, it was only my reflection in the mirror over the long oak bureau. Framed pictures marched along the bureau's top, clearly of the same person as he grew from sullen black-haired little boy to smirking blond man.

"Liam, I presume." As I flipped on the bathroom light, I wondered briefly what had prompted Liam to start dying his hair.

Sofia's pill minder, a long pink plastic box, sat on the pristine white tiles of the vanity. Two of the compartments were already empty, their tops flipped up. The others held two white tablets, a pink oval pill, plus a small gel capsule and a gummy.

"Okay, so I need four pill bottles." When I opened the medicine chest, I took half a heartbeat to admire how orderly the shelves were. I'd been in my house for less than a month and my toiletries had already staged a rave inside the cabinet.

The middle shelf held two orange plastic prescription bottles and a larger brown bottle with the calcium supplements. The larger bottle of multivitamin gummies beneath them on the taller shelf. A small basket on the vanity top held neatly rolled scarlet hand towels, so I removed all but one and used the last to cushion the bottom of the basket, making a nest for the bottles and pill minder.

As I ran out of the bedroom clutching the basket to my chest, I clocked that the wall facing the bed was virtually papered with framed photos of other family members. Even in the gathering dusk, I picked out Ricky's smile immediately, because of course I did, but then I was out the door and down the stairs.

CHAPTER TEN

When I burst out the back door onto the porch, Ricky was still kneeling next to Sofia. As far as I could tell, she hadn't moved. As the door swung shut behind me, I teetered on the edge of the top step for a moment. *Latch the door.* I staggered back and pulled the doorknob until I heard the click, then vaulted off the steps and ran across the lawn.

I dropped down next to Ricky, who was murmuring something to Sofia in Spanish. His phone lay next to him in the damp earth, the screen still lit with the 9-1-1 call.

"Is she conscious?" I asked.

Ricky glanced up at me. "Barely."

"Where's the ambulance?" I gazed around wildly in the deepening dusk. Ambulance companies had minimum response time requirements, but I didn't know what they were here, or where the closest service was located. Granted, Ghost was pretty remote, but medical emergencies could happen anywhere, not to mention fires and—as I had personal experience with—threats of violent crime.

As though the 9-1-1 operator had heard my panic—which she probably had, since the call was on speaker, she said, "The responders will be there in three minutes."

"Maz?" Ricky's voice was hoarse, shaky. I couldn't imagine what he was going through—what the whole clan would go through, should anything happen to Sofia.

"Yeah?"

"Could you do something for me, please?"

"Sure. Anything."

"I have to stay on with the operator. Could you call my mother and let her know what's happening?"

"Absolutely." I pulled out my own phone. "What number?"

"Just call the restaurant and ask for Maria. The nearest hospital is in Richdale, so tell her the family can meet us there."

"You got it."

I stepped away so I wouldn't interfere with the 9-1-1 call and dialed the restaurant.

"Hola. Taqueria Vargas. This is Felicia. How may I help you?"

"Hey, Felicia. This is Maz."

"Maz! I'm *so* excited about taking the trip with Tia. We went shopping in Eugene for the trip today and I talked her into buying a new suitcase. Her old one didn't even have *wheels*. Can you imagine? Thank you *so* much for—"

"Felicia." I felt horrible interrupting and dousing her enthusiasm. "I'm sorry, but is your mom around?"

"Is… is something wrong? It's not Ricky, is it?"

"No. He's fine. But he asked me to speak with your mom."

"She's not here. She had to go pick up some limes at the supermercado in Richdale. From the sound of your voice, this isn't a good thing, but whatever it is, you can tell me."

I glanced back at Ricky and Sofia. He'd probably wanted to spare Felicia hearing about Sofia's collapse from a non-family member, but I decided that speed and efficiency were more necessary than tact at the moment. I hoped they'd all forgive me.

"It's Sofia. She collapsed in the garden."

Felicia gasped. "She's… she's *gone*?"

"No! Not that, but she definitely fainted."

"Her heart?"

"Ricky thinks so. He's with her now and the ambulance is on its way. He wanted me to tell your mom that the family could meet them at the hospital in Richdale."

"Don't worry." All trace of the excited teenager was gone from Felicia's fierce tone. "I'll take care of it. And Maz?"

"Yeah?"

"Thank you. For being there with him."

"Any time."

The call dropped just as the ambulance drove down Birch Street, lights flashing but siren silent. I glanced back at Ricky, who was speaking to Sofia again. I saw her lift a shaking hand and my heart caught in my throat.

The ambulance was pulling up when I stumbled out from between our houses. I ran for the curb, waving both arms, as the engine cut out.

"She's in the back," I called.

The streetlights blinked on as both EMTs climbed out of the vehicle. The driver nodded to me and his partner opened the rear doors and retrieved a bulky kit, slinging the strap over her shoulder. They hurried past me so quickly I had to jog to keep up.

"Ricky?" the woman with the kit called. "Is it Tia? The SVT?"

He nodded. "I think so, but it's worse than I've seen it before. Her heart rate hasn't slowed at all."

"Let's see what's up, shall we?"

She dropped down next to Sofia, and Ricky made way for her partner, scooping up his phone and backing away to stand next to me.

"Hey," I said softly, placing my hand on the small of his back. "You doing all right?" When he shot me a sharp glance, I winced. "Sorry. Stupid question. Of course you're not."

He shook his head. "Not your fault. It's just…" He leaned against me, and I could feel him trembling. "She's always been there, you know? I'm not sure what we'd do without her."

"They'll take care of her."

"I know." He sighed and rested his head on my shoulder, which gave me the courage to wrap my arm around him and pull him closer.

"The female EMT knows you by name. She called Sofia Tia and knew about her condition." I rested my lips against Ricky's hair. "Don't tell me. She's a cousin."

He chuckled weakly. "Not exactly. Her name's Rosalie. She's Nando's girlfriend."

"Nando? From Transitions Transportation?"

Ricky nodded, the top of his head warm against my mouth. "They've been tight since they were kids and got partnered up by their troop leader to sell Girl Scout cookies together." A very delayed mental lightbulb lit up. *Transitions* Transportation. *Ah.* "I'm pretty sure Nando's going to propose, but he's waiting for the perfect moment."

"Warren. We need wheels," Rosalie said.

Rosalie's partner—Warren, presumably—ran back to the ambulance and returned with a gurney, its wheels barely bouncing over the grass because Ricky kept the lawn so smooth. They used a backboard to lift Sofia gently and place her on the mattress.

We followed Rosalie and Warren as they wheeled Sofia toward the street.

"Tell him to do it already."

Ricky glanced at me, clearly torn between listening to me and watching the EMTs lift Sofia into the ambulance.

"Nando. Tell him to do it." I thought of Avi and Oren. Of Oren's plans for the Canadian wedding that never had a chance to take place. "Any moment is perfect if it means you get to spend it with the ones you love."

He held my gaze for an instant and then gave a sharp nod before moving into the street. The light from inside the ambulance washed over him, casting unexpected shadows under his cheekbones.

Warren started to close the doors, but Rosalie held up a hand to stall him and looked down at us.

"Ricky? You riding along?"

"Yes." He lunged forward, but paused before he could step onto the bumper and looked back at me. "I don't want to ask more of you."

"It's fine. Whatever you need."

He pulled his keys out of his jacket pocket, teased one out with the tips of his fingers, and used it to hold the whole jangling bunch out to me. "This is for Tia's house. Could you lock up for me, please? The outside lights are on a timer, but—"

"I've got it." I gently took the keyring from him. "Do you want me to bring your truck to the hospital for you?"

He shook his head. "No. There'll be enough of the family there to give me a ride, and I don't know how long we'll be."

"You'll keep me updated?"

He nodded, and then climbed up into the ambulance, taking a seat next to Sofia's feet while Rosalie did something official near her head.

Warren closed the rear doors. "Thanks for your help."

"No problem."

He jogged toward the front of the ambulance, and a moment later, the engine turned over.

I stepped up onto the grass verge as they pulled away, rubbing my chest absently. It felt... hollow. Like something precious had been uprooted and nothing planted in its place. If anything happened to Sofia, I expected Ricky's entire family would be feeling the same or worse.

The ambulance turned onto Main Street and its flashing lights disappeared behind the dark bulk of Patrice's house and trees.

"Will she be okay?" Avi's voice held the kind of worry I'd only heard from him a couple of times before.

"I hope so. She—"

Wait. *Avi?*

I whipped my head around. "How did you— When—" I took a breath. "You're outside."

Avi blinked and looked down at himself, then turned in a slow circle, surveying the street, the Manor grounds, Sofia's house, *our* house.

"I am." He met my gaze. "How do you suppose I got here?"

"You don't know?"

He gave me his patented Avi can't-believe-you're-being-this-dense look from under his brows, chin tilted down, hair flopping over his forehead. "We've been over this, Maz. I don't know how *any* of this works."

"Maybe your, I don't know, range is expanding or something."

"I... suppose that could be. It's just as likely as anything else."

I glanced at the corner again. There was no sign of the ambulance, and I had no idea how long it would be until I had more news about Sofia. However, I knew one thing for certain.

There was zero chance I'd be able to focus on any task that required responsible adult decisions, such as sorting through the many, *many* boxes in my house—both mine and Oren's.

I straightened my shoulders and met Avi's gaze. "Then what do you say we experiment?"

CHAPTER ELEVEN

"Okay, then." I stowed Ricky's keys in my hoodie pocket, propped my fists on my hips, and looked up at our house, the streetlight casting my shadow on the grass. "How should we do this? We know you can make it from the house to the street."

Avi matched my pose, but of course had no shadow. "Maybe we should circle the house? See if I can access all of the grounds?"

"Good idea."

When I'd arrived in Ghost and got my first look at the house, I'd paced around it, half in awe and half in annoyance that the door locks were stuffed with sawdust and I couldn't get inside. I hadn't walked the entire yard then. For one thing, it was enormous, and for another, it lacked features of interest, such as Sofia's garden and natty scarecrow.

My yard and Professor DeHaven's had the same gentle downward slope as Sofia's. Mine had a few widely spaced trees, all neatly pruned—no doubt Ricky's handiwork. Patrice, however, was evidently as minimalist in her landscaping as she was with her communication, because other than the Doug firs that guarded her property line along Main Street, her lawn was just a smooth expanse of green, all the way down to seasonal creek burbling past the three houses.

Since we were testing for distance limits, we kept to the perimeter, starting on the west side. Nothing physical marked the boundary, though, so we were just guessing that the property line was about halfway between our house and Patrice's.

We skirted the edge of the gravel drive that ended at the garage and continued past the rear wall of the house. I glanced sidelong at Avi.

"Feeling anything?"

He shot me a glare, but I noticed that he was clutching the hem of his cardigan with both hands. "It's the first time I've seen the house from outside in more than ten years, Maz. What do you think?"

I winced. "Sorry." I was thinking more about ghost manifestation stuff rather than, you know, *feelings*. "Do you want me to leave you alone for a bit before we go on?"

His shoulders rose and fell. "No. I'm sorry too. I didn't mean to snap." His mouth lifted in—yeah, sue me—a ghost of a smile. "I'll have time enough to wallow in messy emotions later."

"All right then." I pointed to Patrice's window. "Did I ever tell you that on my first day here, when I was still trying to get past your sawdust trap—"

"Sorry about that."

"It's cool." As a matter of fact, Avi's sawdust manipulation skills had more than one upside. Not only had it eventually saved my life, but it had introduced me to Ricky. So, you know. No regrets.

We walked past the bulkhead and down the lawn toward the creek. According to Taryn, our official plot extended to the poplars that edged the green space behind the old elementary school. However, Avi's family, as well as Patrice and Sofia, treated the creek as the de facto property line. Judging by the neatly trimmed grass on the other side, though, I suspect Ricky maintained it just as he did our three lawns.

Avi paused next to a tree about ten feet tall with dark green oblong leaves about the length of my hand. "This is a black tulip magnolia. It was just a sapling... then. We intended to plant several fruit trees down here after Oren—" His voice caught. "After Oren moved in, but that was in the summer, and we needed to wait for January to plant the bare root stock."

"Would you... That is, I don't want to step on your toes, or bring up any bad memories, but would you like to do that? Plant some fruit trees? This January?"

Avi lowered his head for a moment. "I... I would like that." When he looked up, the back porch light reflected off his glasses so I couldn't see his eyes, but the tone of his voice told me everything I needed to know.

Hell, yeah, we're planting those trees.

"Why don't you show me where you'd like them while we continue our tour?"

He shook his head, chuckling. "It's barely May, Maz. I think we have time."

"I know." I tracked the toe of my Converse as it traced a circle in the grass. "But coming here, inheriting this house from an uncle I never knew—"

"Third cousin," Avi said.

I froze, my gaze snapping to Avi. "What?"

Avi's brow wrinkled. "What what?"

"You said third cousin."

"Yes." He drew out the word with exaggerated patience. "Your mother was his second cousin once removed, which makes you his third cousin."

"I am. But I'm pretty sure we never talked about the relationship. How did you know?"

"Because Oren told me you'd be next in line when he made her his contingent benef— Oh."

Yeah. Oh.

"You knew." My lungs were suddenly full of lead. "About me. You both knew about me before."

Avi reached out with one transparent hand. "Maz. My memories aren't complete. I can't even remember what's supposed to be on the shelves in my house. This doesn't mean anything."

"Did you, Avi?" My voice sounded like it was at the bottom of a barrel through the roaring in my ears. "Did you know?"

"You have to understand. We were drawing up our wills. Saul told us that even though we were leaving everything to each other, we should have contingent beneficiaries in case of... well, in case. My fallback was actually Richdale University, since I didn't have any family that was especially close. Oren laughed."

"He *laughed* at me?"

"No! I didn't— That wasn't—" Avi pushed his glasses up and rubbed his eyes. "He said he could do better than a university. He actually had somebody he wanted to *benefit*. A cousin." He kept trying to catch my gaze, but I kept slipping the hook. "Second cousin once removed."

That hit me square in the solar plexus. "My mom. Not me. He left everything to my mom."

"If her name was Laura Brandon, then yes. Your last name is different, so I didn't realize at first that you were her son."

"She didn't change her name when she married my dad." The sound I made might qualify as a laugh if you'd never heard one before. "He always joked that he thought about changing his, but having two Lauras in the family would be too confusing."

"Oren said she was the only person in their entire family who didn't revile him when he came out, so he wanted to thank her. He left her a small bequest originally, too, although he said it had more sentimental value. Something from their childhoods, I think."

The roaring in my ears intensified, and I had to brace my hands on my knees. I'd seen Oren's will. Taryn showed it to me when we were finalizing probate. My mom's name wasn't on it.

Mine was.

I was so overwhelmed at the time, it hadn't occurred to me what that meant, but now I connected those dots: Oren had altered the will after she died, which meant he'd known of her death, known about me, but had never reached out.

Yeah, he was suffering his own debilitating loss. But we could have *helped* each other. *Why?* Why had he left me alone?

Maybe someday, if Avi's dreams came true and Oren joined him here in ghostly communion, I could pose that question to him. While I sincerely hoped that day would come for Avi's sake, I wasn't all that eager for it to arrive for my own.

It was probably a good thing that ghosts weren't punchable. At least not yet.

"Maz?" Avi's tone was tentative. "Are you okay?"

Honestly? No. But what Oren did or did not do wasn't Avi's fault, particularly since he'd died three years before my parents. So I pushed myself upright and shook my hair back.

"Let's keep going."

We finished the circuit of our property. Avi didn't glitch at all, although he didn't say much. Neither did I, for that matter. It wasn't exactly a night for cheerful banter.

By the time we reached the street again, my emotions had more or less leveled out. I pulled out my phone, just in case I'd missed a text from Ricky when I'd been having my little existential breakdown, but there was nothing.

I really wished there had been something.

"Okay." I tucked my phone away. "It looks like you've got the full run of the house and yard." I gestured to Sofia's house. "I need to lock up next door. Want to see if you can visit the neighbors, too? You were friends with Sofia, weren't you?"

He scoffed. "*Everybody* was friends with Sofia. Or I suppose it's more accurate to say that Sofia was friends with everybody. Her warmth was irresistible."

"Is."

"What?"

"Her warmth *is* irresistible."

"Ah. Right." He gazed up at the second-floor window nearest my house, which I now knew was Liam's suite. "The only people who could resist her charm were her son's in-laws."

"Liam's mother's family, you mean? The Frosts?"

"Yes. They were… very White, if you get my drift. I was actually surprised that Susanne bucked her family's pressure enough to marry Lorenzo."

"She had a backbone, eh?"

"Not really. I think she was used to always getting her way, her parents were used to letting her have it, and Lorenzo was… very handsome. Then Lorenzo proved he had more business savvy than his father-in-law and took the company to whole other level." He smiled wryly. "Apparently, for his ability to generate buckets of cash, they were able to overlook his ethnicity, although they refused to call him anything but *Lawrence* until the end."

"I thought the company closed."

"It did. But that was after Lorenzo died." Avi chewed on his lower lip as he gazed up at Sofia's house. "He had a bad heart, too. If Sofia—"

"Hey." Not for the first time, I regretted that I couldn't actually *touch* Avi enough to pat his shoulder. "Ricky told me Lorenzo was definitely Type A, which brings a certain set of stressors. Sofia's condition is different. It's more electrical than anything else. Come on." I beckoned to him. "Let's go lock up."

I strode toward Sofia's front porch, but when I got to the door, I realized Avi wasn't with me. When I turned around, he hadn't moved. He was staring at the ground in front of his feet. I hurried back to him.

"Can't you cross the boundary? Do you need to be invited? I'm not sure if I can—"

He glanced up at me irritably. "I'm a ghost, not a vampire, Maz. It's just… It's a big step, okay? And for an instant, there, something… wobbled."

"Is it still, er, wobbling?"

"No." He ran both hands through his hair. I noted that they were trembling. "No. It's fine now."

"If it will make it any easier, I'll stay right by your side."

Something I couldn't identify flickered across his face. "I'd appreciate that. Thanks." His chest expanded with a huge breath. "I wonder if this is what prisoners feel when they're finally released and walk through the gates." He lifted his chin and took a step forward. "Huh."

I tucked my thumbs into my front pockets. "A little anticlimactic?"

"Yes and no." He angled his head toward Sofia's house. "Shall we?"

"Let's."

We walked up the porch steps together. I pulled Ricky's keys out of my hoodie pocket and sorted through them. "I *think* I remember which one is Sofia's house key, but—"

"Just try the knob, Maz. Sofia never locked her doors before. I can't imagine things have changed so much in as little as ten years."

"You don't know Ricky," I muttered. "He'd probably come over and lock them himself if she didn't follow proper security protocol." However, when I tried the door, it opened. I glanced over at Avi. "Let's not tell him about this. I don't want to get Sofia in trouble."

Avi canted an eyebrow. "Even if I were inclined to tattle, how exactly do you imagine I could? He can't hear me."

"Ah. Right. Good point."

I thought about the EVP equipment I'd ordered earlier. Sheesh, was it only this afternoon? It felt like it had been days since Ricky and I had gotten home to Avi's panicked appearance. If everything worked out, pretty soon Avi would have a way to tattle on anybody he wanted.

I could only hope.

CHAPTER TWELVE

While I waited on the scarlet rug bordered with a spiky geometric pattern in deep blue and green in the entry, Avi stood frozen in the doorway, eyes wide and lips slightly parted.

I cleared my throat. "Want to step inside?"

He startled. "Oh. Sorry. It's just... I *remember* now." He glanced at my hand holding the edge of the door. "You could probably just close that through me, you know."

"Maybe. But that seems rude."

He stepped out of the way and drifted toward the living room. Once he'd cleared the door, I shut it and made sure it was fully latched and that the deadbolt was thrown. Ricky had told me about the timer, and I didn't want to screw up the schedule, so I didn't switch off the porch light.

When I joined Avi, he was standing in the middle of the living room, his eyes closed, his chest rising and falling in a slow, deliberate rhythm. "Her house always smelled so good," he murmured. "She loved to cook for family and friends."

"Loves," I said.

He opened his eyes, brow furrowed. "What?"

"She *loves* to cook for family and friends," I said through gritted teeth.

Avi grimaced. "Yes. Sorry."

"And the house still smells amazing."

"Maz. Please." He lifted a hand toward me, but stopped, his fingers curling as though he'd just remembered that he couldn't actually touch me. "I didn't mean to upset you. And I certainly didn't mean to imply that Sofia won't be perfectly fine. But understand, from my perspective, this house, her cooking, the times Oren and I sat around her table—all of that is in the past." He glanced away. "Just like me."

I told the storm around my heart to settle down. Sofia would be *fine*, and I could scarcely blame Avi for seeing things through a decade-old lens.

"Um... Can you smell anything now?"

He shook his head. "No more than I can at our house, which is to say, not at all." He turned to me, hope flickering in his expression. "Could we... That is, I know you're only here to lock up, but would you mind if we walked around a little in here?"

"Weeelll." I shifted from foot to foot, clenching the keys in my fist. "I don't want to creep around in here like a, well, creeper. Or snoop like—"

"A snooper?" he said with a half-smile. "I don't want to *snoop*. I just want to discover the *memories*. If you recall, I couldn't even remember what should have been in my own house until I saw it. If I can..." He made a helpless gesture. "I don't know how to explain it. It's not exactly priming the pump. I mean, I can look at that picture—" He pointed to yet another framed photo of Liam that hung right next to an icon of the Virgin Mary and squinted. "Hunh. When did Liam start dying his hair?"

"I don't kn—"

"Never mind. But see, that's what I'm talking about. Until I saw that, I didn't remember that Liam used to have hair as black as Ricky's. But that photo... It's like it filled in a blank spot on my mental gallery wall, and now I remember what Liam looked like when he was a surly nineteen-year-old, the last time he visited Sofia before I, well, wasn't around to see him anymore."

"That may have been the last time he was here. Ricky told me he doesn't visit much, especially after he started college."

Avi snorted. "I'm shocked he managed to find a college he deemed worthy of his valuable matriculation."

"Harvard," I said, deadpan.

"Eh." Avi waved a dismissive hand. "If you can't manage Oxford, I suppose it's *adequate*."

"Says the guy who went to the University of Oregon."

He didn't rise to the bait. "Actually, it was my first choice. I landed my agent with a story I wrote in my junior year and paid off all my student loans with the royalties from the first Harcourt and Corchran book."

"Hey." I held up my hands. "I've never graduated from anywhere, so all respect, man."

He tilted his head, the lift of his eyebrows like a question mark. "Never? I'm surprised, considering how advanced your writing skills are."

I shrugged. "I left U Conn when my parents were killed. I tried to get back into student mode a couple of times—PSU was the last attempt, which is how I ended up in Portland. My folks didn't leave me much money, though, and student loans are the worst, so my academic career just kind of"—I made a rolling motion with one hand—"folded. Inertia. What can I say?"

"You don't need to justify yourself to me, Maz. I was just surprised, that's all." He turned toward the kitchen, his expression wistful. "Could we go in there next?"

"Let's leave that for last, since that's the best route to the back door and we'll have to lock up. Come on." I jerked my thumb toward the stairs. "I don't remember leaving lights on upstairs, but I wasn't actually firing on all synapses at the time, so I need to retrace my steps."

In case Ricky tried to contact me, I kept my phone in my hand as we meandered at Avi-discovery pace through Sofia's house. We didn't spend much time upstairs, although he did snort and mutter, "Typical," when he peeked into Liam's man-suite. Downstairs, while he was fascinated by Sofia's meticulously organized crafting room, it was the kitchen where he lingered the longest. I gave up trying to read the expressions on his face, because he was clearly going through some things.

Hanging more memories in his mental gallery walls.

I didn't rush him, just leaned against the counter and stared at my phone, but I wasn't able to conjure up a message from Ricky with the power of my glare.

"All right," Avi said softly. "We can go now."

We walked onto the back porch, its light illuminating the yard enough that I could make out the crushed tomato plants and the hollow in the soil where Sofia had lain.

It took me three tries to get the door to latch because my hand slipped off the doorknob twice.

When I caught up with Avi, he was standing on the lawn, halfway down the slope between the house and the garden, gazing up at the night sky.

"I can see stars from the attic windows, but it looks different from out here."

I looked up, spotting Ursa Major right away. Ghost didn't have the kind of light pollution that Portland or even McMinnville or Hillsboro did, and since the moon wasn't up, the sky was pretty glorious. "Yeah. It does."

We walked slowly toward our house, but when I started up the back porch steps, Avi didn't follow me. I turned to look down at him. His shoulders were hunched under his shapeless cardigan and his hands were shoved deep in its front pockets.

"You okay?"

"Do you mind…" He swallowed. "That is, I'd like to stay out here for a while longer, if that's okay."

I stepped back onto the grass. "Avi. We started out as involuntary housemates, but I like to think we're finding our way to mutually agreeable cohabitation. That doesn't mean we don't need our own space now and then. Take all the time you want." I smiled and tried not to let my gaze drift to Sofia's garden. "I won't even give you a curfew."

He laughed softly. "I appreciate it."

I turned and mounted the steps, but when my hand was on the doorknob, I heard him murmur, "Thank you. For everything."

I pretended I didn't hear and stepped inside, closing the door softly behind me. "I'm pretty sure I'm the one who should be thanking you for everything."

If it wasn't for Avi and Uncle Oren—okay, third cousin Oren, and I *still* had some *feelings* about him not contacting me during his lifetime, considering he'd put me in his freaking *will*—I wouldn't have this house. I wouldn't have a *home*. I wouldn't have enough disposable income to send my neighbor on the trip of her dreams. I wouldn't have a fascinating job or raft of new friends or a potential boyfriend. A potential boyfriend who *still* hadn't—

My cell phone vibrated, and I inhaled slowly when I checked the screen because it was a text from Ricky at last. Although it hadn't been much more than an hour since the ambulance pulled away. Maybe I should cut potential boyfriend a little slack.

R: *Tia in with doctor now. Waiting with family so can't call.*

M: *Will she be okay?*

R: *They're keeping her overnight at least, but they think so. I'll call tomorrow.*

M: *Okay. If they let you see her, give her my love.*

R: *Will do.*

I sighed, briefly considering making myself a cup of tea, but couldn't rustle up the effort. I wandered through the kitchen and family room. When I got to the vestibule, Avi suddenly popped into view next to me.

I staggered back a step, grabbing the newel post to regain my balance. "I thought you wanted to stay outside."

He looked down at himself and then over his shoulder at the front door. "I did. I was. And then I was here."

"Maybe you ran out of ghost juice or something? The longest I've ever seen you manifest is about an hour, but that's only within my sightlines. Can you hang around for longer than that?"

He scowled at me. "I don't exactly set a timer on myself."

I sighed. "Look, Avi. I get that it hasn't been a great day for either of us, but I'm trying to help, all right?"

He clenched his eyes shut and rubbed one hand across his forehead. "Sorry. I know. But it's so *frustrating*. I don't know anything about my... my *condition*, and I don't even know what I don't know."

I heard a muffled meow from behind me and turned to find Gil prancing down the stairs with one of my tube socks in his mouth. He dropped it at my feet and looked up, expecting his due of praise. I complied.

"Yes." I knelt down and skritched his ears and under his chin. "You are the mightiest hunter in all the land."

Avi hunkered down next to me and because he never missed a chance with one of the only things he could touch, he stroked along Gil's back, lifting the fur there as usual. "Has he ever actually caught something?"

"Oh, trust me. He's got moves. The only reason Greg didn't have a mouse problem at his condo is because Gil caught them and I disposed of them before Greg got home from work." In fact, I suspected he'd discovered a "problem" since then—I'd spotted the fancy electronic mousetraps in the corners of the great room and bedroom when Ricky and I had been there to pick up my stuff. "When Taryn first contacted me and told me I'd inherited a house, I was afraid we'd arrive at some rat-infested hovel. So if you're responsible for rodent control as well as dust control, thank you for that."

"You're welcome." Avi might have used the absent dust to dry out his tone. "I'd be more impressed with myself if I knew how I did it."

"I think Gil was disappointed in their absence, but if we don't let on you're the culprit, I suspect he'll forgive you." I picked up the sock. "Although it hurts his pride that he's reduced to capturing my laundry. Oh, and this." I dug Oren's ring out of my pocket. "I think he probably knocked that bowl where you keep it off its shelf. He was batting this around when Ricky and I got in. Sorry. I'll put it—"

"No!" Avi clutched at my wrist, his hand passing through my arm and leaving the ache of remembered cold behind it. "Wait."

I fought the urge to shove my hand in my pocket to warm it up. "Okay. What's up?"

"This is it, Maz. This is what we've been looking for." He lifted his gaze to my face, his eyes shining. "This is the answer."

CHAPTER THIRTEEN

"The answer?" I tucked my hand against my chest to warm it up. "Okay, I'll bite. What was the question?"

Avi rolled his eyes. "Why I can go outside."

I waggled my fingers at the floor. "You're not outside now."

"Yes." A verbal eyeroll this time. "Because the ring is inside."

"The ring?" I lowered my hand, uncurled my fingers, and stared at Oren's wedding band. "You think the ring has some kind of unlocking mechanism? I'd think a key would—"

"Not the ring by itself." Avi huffed and ran both hands through his hair. "Look. Could you humor me for a minute?"

"Sure. Anything you want."

He pointed to the Mission-style console table that sat inside the front door. "Put the ring there, please."

I did, much to Gil's interest. I pointed at him. "You are not to touch this." He gave me a slow blink.

"Don't worry about him," Avi said, shooing me toward the front door. "If he steals it, I'll watch where it goes."

"If you say so." I opened the door and walked out onto the front porch. "Is this far enough?"

He nodded, his chin set determinedly. He paced toward the door, but when he tried to step over the threshold, he blinked back to the foot of the stairs where he'd been before, startling Gil into bouncing away sideways.

Okay. That was... interesting.

He beckoned to me. "Now come back and get the ring." I did. "Back outside, please?"

I stepped onto the porch.

He joined me. We met each other's eyes. I don't know which one of us started to laugh first, but suddenly we were both doubled over. Which was a good thing, because that meant I was in the perfect position to grab Gil when he made a dash for the lawn.

"Oh, no you don't." I set him inside and closed the door. When I turned, Avi was standing under the maple tree, gazing up through the leaves. I leaned against the porch rail, watching him. "So. Got any ideas on why the ring is the thing?"

He nodded. "I do. Not sure you'll like them."

"Hit me."

"Well…" He lowered his gaze from the leaves and met my eyes. "You're a little bit Oren."

I held up my thumb and forefinger, a hairsbreadth between them. "A very little bit. A third cousin bit."

"Maybe that's all it takes. Maybe that's why I can talk to you and no one else. I could *always* talk to Oren. About anything. Even that last time, when I… When we…" Avi's chest heaved and his voice dropped to a whisper. "When we fought. I still told him all the reasons *why* I was so upset and he didn't dismiss my feelings. We never hid anything from each other."

I glanced down at the ring gleaming in my palm. "Except this."

"Yes." He moved to the foot of the steps. "Except that."

Oren hadn't told Avi about the plans for a trip to Canada to get married, but I think we could both give him a pass on that one. You could hardly spill the beans on a big wonderful surprise if you wanted it to stay, you know, a big wonderful surprise.

"If it's the ring plus me, though, why did you blink inside earlier?"

He shrugged. "Maybe there's a proximity limit? We can test later."

"Good idea. I think we should test to see if it works with somebody else holding the ring, too. Somebody you and Oren both knew and trusted."

"That would probably be Ricky or Saul."

I winced. "Yeah. Ricky's probably got a little too much on his mind right now. Saul and Jerry are out of town until Monday."

"We can wait on that." He spread his arms. "For now, this is enough." He ducked his head and peered up at me, almost shyly. "Maybe tomorrow we could take a walk down Main Street?"

"Of course." I turned my head toward the corner, my gaze sweeping across the wrought iron palings that marched along the edge of the Manor grounds, and my jaw sagged.

Wait just a freaking minute.

An ember ignited in my middle and I took the steps two at a time to join him. I *really* wished I could touch him because I wanted to grab his hands and dance down the slate walk.

"You said you were frustrated because you don't know anything about your afterlife, right?"

"We've been over this," he said, his verbal eyeroll accompanied by its physical equivalent. "Multiple times."

"Yeah, yeah." I couldn't fight my grin. "You know who *might* know something about that?"

He crossed his arms. "I'm not in the mood for guessing games, Maz."

"Humor me, okay?" I crept past him on the balls of my feet, and, just as I hoped, he pivoted to follow until I was facing the porch and he was facing Iris Lane. "Tell me, Avi. Who once lived right across the street from our house?"

"I told you. No guessing ga—" He blinked. "Oh."

"Exactly! Thaddeus Richdale spent the last half of his life poking at the veil, and I just happen to be employed in organizing the boatload of detritus from his explorations. So what do you think?"

"What do I think about what?"

I grinned, rocking from my toes to my heels. "Come with me. Help me go through Thaddeus's stuff."

He pointed to my hand, which still held Oren's ring. "In case you've forgotten, I can't even pick up my husband's ring."

"Yes, but you're aces with paper."

His eyebrows shot up. "I... I'm not sure I would say I've reached *aces* status yet."

"But your paper handling muscles are getting stronger every day, and Thaddeus's stuff is about eighty percent paper. With the two of us working on it, we'll be able to sort through the... the dross and find the gold much faster."

He didn't completely lose his scowl, but there was a definite twinkle in his eye—unless that was just the porch light shining through from behind him. "Aren't you afraid you'll lose your job if you finish too quickly?"

"Nah. I always knew this was a temporary gig, and I'm not drawing it out to soak Saul and the Manor for more money just to line my own pockets."

"Is this your clever ploy to avoid sorting through it on your own?"

"That's not it either. I don't *mind* going through everything. I told you. It's fascinating. But I'm used to modern search engines and data retrieval protocols, which boxes of dusty papers and mysterious arcane items definitely do not have. If we can get answers sooner, not only will it help the Manor, it'll help you. And it'll help the town, too."

"How do you figure that?"

"In my first few days here, Jerry told me about the annual parade and festival, and how it had gotten cut back and finally canceled because of lack of attendance." I gestured for Avi to follow me as I trotted up the porch steps. "I think that reduction was a mistake. Instead of going smaller, you should have gone bigger."

Avi trailed behind me as I opened the door and deftly snagged Gil before he could dodge outside. "I wasn't exactly in a position to do anything about it at all, considering I was already dead."

"I meant *you* as in the town, not you personally." I closed the door, and with Gil in my arms, headed into the library and plopped onto the window seat. He sat opposite me. "Paranormal tourism is a huge thing, Avi. There are legend tripping conferences. Self-guided haunted site crawls. Guided tours."

When I'd been looking at EVP equipment today, I'd found multiple companies promoting them, but they were focused on *finding* ghosts. If we could reverse engineer the process—from the presence of an actual ghost backward to how the ghost arrived and chose to manifest—we could put Ghost on the paranormal map.

We could save the town.

CHAPTER FOURTEEN

From a combination of worry and anticipation, I passed a restless night. When I woke up with Gil curled next to my hip, the sky beyond the bedroom was fading from gray to, well, lighter gray. At this time of year, a month or so from the solstice, that meant that we were barely past five.

Ordinarily, provided Gil wasn't feeling particularly peckish and insisting on an early breakfast, I'd snatch another hour or so of sleep. But today I knew better than to try. I'd only end up staring at the ceiling with visions of how everything could change, for both better and worse. So, careful not to disturb Gil, I eased out from under the blankets and headed for the bathroom.

Gil was still snuggled in his blanket nest when I emerged after stumbling through my shower and morning grooming routine, observing me out of one slitted eye as I stepped into a pair of sweatpants.

"I know." I pulled a long-sleeved Henley over my head. "I'm shocked too. But what can I tell you? Things to do and fingernails to bite." I grabbed the edge of the blankets and gave them a shake. "Coming?"

He made his opinion clear by engaging in the longest stretch in the history of cats, with all his claws extended, before he hopped onto the floor with a very sarcastic tail twitch and deigned to let me make the bed.

By the time I padded downstairs barefoot, Gil had recovered from his snit and galloped ahead of me, disappearing into the family room in a flash of ginger fur. I peered into the library before I followed him. The dim room seemed empty, but in this house, you never knew.

"Avi?"

No response, and I didn't detect the telltale glimmer of Avi's body on the window seat, where we'd sat last night debating where to keep Oren's ring. Now that we knew it had more than sentimental value, we didn't want to leave it anywhere it might be subject to accidental loss—aka Gil's penchant for shiny things.

I wasn't about to wear it on my finger—Avi and I both cringed at that notion.

We'd settled on threading it onto a short, sturdy stainless steel chain that one of my previous boyfriends had used to attach his water bottle to his backpack on his week-long wilderness hikes. Yeah, that relationship hadn't lasted beyond the first time he'd convinced me to come with him. Even so, we'd parted on fairly good terms, acknowledging that our interests just didn't align. He'd left me the water bottle though: "Just in case you ever want to give hiking another try."

I had not.

That water bottle had gotten lost somewhere in the multiple moves after my parents died, but the chain had survived, passing from laptop bag to laptop bag through the years.

We'd then locked the ring in the desk drawer because we wanted to use it *intentionally*, rather than have me carry it around all the time. Besides, Gil didn't present the only loss threat, if you take my meaning. Remember the disappearing water bottle? Yeah, that.

We hadn't conducted any more tests last night. Avi was more than a little overwhelmed by our discovery, so after we'd secured the ring, he'd vanished. This morning, though, we had plans. Big plans.

Plans that would be much more successful if I were fully awake and focused.

So I switched on the electric kettle and chose the tea with *all* the caffeine. As I was waiting for the water to heat, my phone vibrated on the counter. I exhaled gustily when I saw it was a text from Ricky. *Please be good news, please be good news.*

R: Tia better this morning. Family's still here.

Good news. Thank goodness.

M: All of them?

Ricky responded with a laugh emoji. Hunh. I'd never thought of Ricky as an emoji kind of guy, but even though my question hadn't been a joke—not intentionally, anyway—I took this as a good sign about Ricky's state of mind, and therefore about Sofia's prognosis. The tension I hadn't lost overnight eased and my shoulders relaxed about ten percent.

R: The hospital is used to us.
M: Let me guess—you've got a cousin who works there.

Another laugh emoji.

R: Charge nurse. So they're letting us in to see her a few at a time.
M: Any diagnosis yet?
R: Waiting on lab results. Could you do me a favor?
M: Sure.
R: Water Tia's garden please?
M: No problem.
R: Thanks! Hose bib on the back of the garage.

Garage. Ha! I knew where that was now.

M: On it.

I waited a moment, but nothing else popped up on the screen, so I scooped a spoonful of loose tea out of the box, ready to dump it into the tea basket. The phone vibrated again, and I grinned as I leaned over to read the notification.

A heart emoji. Ricky had texted me a heart emoji.

I scrabbled the phone off the counter and stood there, staring at the screen, tea leaves pattering onto the counter as the tea scoop tilted in my hand.

"Maz?"

I jerked my head up at the concern in Avi's voice. He was standing right at my elbow and I flailed, the rest of the tea going airborne. "Unh?"

"Is something wrong? Is it Sofia?"

"Look at this!" I thrust the phone at Avi's face.

He reared back. "I'm farsighted and presbyopic, Maz. I can't read anything that close to my nose." He shoved his glasses up with a knuckle. "Or in my nose, for that matter. Best keep the minimum safe distance so I don't fry your phone."

"Right. Sorry." I gingerly placed the phone on the counter. "Sofia's doing better. That's not the issue. It's this." I tapped the last message from Ricky. "What does it mean?"

Avi frowned, bending over the screen with his hands clasped behind his back. "It's a heart."

"I *know* it's a heart, but what does it mean? Is it, like, gratitude? Appreciation? Support? Or… or…"

"Maz." Avi straightened and faced me. "You're overthinking this."

"I am?" I winced. "Crap, I am."

"You know how fond I am of you and Ricky, so I'm saying this with the deepest affection. You're both idiots."

I blinked. "Wow. Harsh."

"Not at all. Simply a realistic observation from a friend. You're not in middle school. If you want to know what it means, *ask him*. And if you want something more from your relationship, *tell him*. If I know one thing about Ricky Vargas, it's that he doesn't have a cruel bone in his body. If he doesn't want more from you, he'll tell you. If he might, but he's not ready yet, then wait for him." He narrowed his eyes and his voice dropped into a register that would be a big hit in a they're-calling-from-inside-the-house slasher movie. "You think he's worth waiting for, don't you?"

"Of course he is. Of course I do."

"Well, then. There's no problem, is there?" Avi stepped back, dusting his palms together. "My job here is done."

"You should start a business," I grumbled as I gathered the scattered tea leaves. "Relationship advice from beyond the veil."

"I'll take it under advisement," he said placidly. "What's our plan?"

"I promised Ricky I'd water Sofia's garden." I managed to get tea into the basket and the basket into the cup this time. Steam rose as I poured water over the tea and set it aside to steep. "Do you feel like coming outside with me while I do that? Then we could test the proximity limits. See how far away you can be from me before you get snapped back to the house."

Avi rubbed his chest absently. "Okay."

I studied his face, where a crease had formed between his brows as though he were in pain but hadn't realized it yet. "Is something the matter?"

"What? Why do you think—" He looked down at his hand. "Oh. No. Nothing at the moment. But do you remember last night when I had that... that *moment* on Sofia's front lawn?"

There were a lot of *moments* last night, but I forbore from asking *which one*. "You mean when you said something wobbled?"

He nodded. "A pull in my chest. Not pain, precisely. More like the strain you feel on a muscle when you're just about to overdo it. I thought it was just overwhelm from the new experience, but maybe it was a warning that I was too far from the ring."

"That's... concerning." I leaned my elbows on the counter and propped my chin on my fists. "It could be a good thing. A cue that we need to reposition ourselves. Although I'm not crazy about the idea that the connection *could* be overdone. If we strain it too much, push too far, will it injure you permanently?"

"Like I said." He spread his hands. "We don't know what we don't know. All we can do is experiment."

"Okay then." My tea had finally reached an acceptable strength, so I set aside the basket and took a cautious sip. *Ah.* Just this side of tongue-scalding and with enough tannin to make me fight a pucker. Perfect. "I don't have a specific clock-in time at the Manor, especially since Saul is still in Victoria, so we can afford to spend some time testing this morning, especially since we're up so early. Do you want to head down Main Street?"

He shook his head. "Maybe this evening. Oren and I—" He took a breath and very deliberately placed both palms on the countertop. "Oren and I used to love to walk down Main Street at twilight."

Once again, I wished I could touch Avi so I could pat his shoulder or his hand to offer support and encouragement. Right on cue, Gil jumped up on the counter and sauntered over to sit between Avi's hands.

Avi smiled crookedly. "I don't suppose Gil can come outside with us?"

"Only if he's in his carrier, which is not his favorite thing. Granted, we don't have a lot of traffic around here, but Gil has no concept that cars are higher on the food chain than he is."

"Maybe you should invest in one of those mesh pet tents." Avi stroked Gil's back. "He might appreciate the change in scenery as much as I do."

I raised my eyebrows. "That's... not a bad idea." I'd seen those tents—and the tubes that you could get to attach to them

—but I'd never lived anyplace I could use them. "I'll check up on that tonight."

Avi grinned at me. "Use the royalty money on it, Maz. With no guilt. I owe it to Gil in return for what he gives me." His grin faded a bit, turning into a fond smile as he gazed down at Gil. "Connection."

Well. I could hardly argue about that.

"Consider it done." I set my tea mug on the counter. "I'll change quickly and we can head outside. If you're ready."

"More than."

I ran upstairs to change into gardening clothes. When I came back down, I detoured into the library to collect the ring. The chain was long enough that I could fasten it around my belt loop and still tuck the ring deep into my pocket for double protection.

When I returned to the kitchen, Avi was still petting Gil, but he was gazing out the window at the brightening day. I cleared my throat, and he shifted his attention back to me.

"Ideally," I said, "I'd like to check vertical limits as well as horizontal distance, but there's no point in trying that now because you've already got full access inside the house and I'm not about to climb a tree. But maybe we can test it at the Manor later. It's got levels and angles galore."

"Sounds reasonable." He gestured to me. "Since I can't open the door, the next step is on you."

That made me pause. "Do you think you could walk through the door if it was closed and I was on the other side?"

Avi's brows disappeared behind the frames of his glasses. "Yes and no?"

"Meaning?"

"It's logistics, I suppose." He held his hand out flat, palm toward the floor. "To get from here"—he slid his palm forward and stopped—"to here, I don't need to physically traverse the whole path. I just go from here"—he waggled his fingers—"to here." He held up the other hand and dropped the first. "So it doesn't matter what's in my way. Because nothing *is* in my way."

"But I've watched you climb stairs and walk from room to room." I gestured to the window. "Outside last night, you kept pace with me the whole time."

He shrugged. "I think it has more to do with my location relative to others and their expectations, and, I don't know, muscle memory?"

"If that's the case…" I squinted, tapping a finger on my chin. "Okay. First test. I'll go out onto the porch and close the door. You join me as soon as you can."

I stepped outside. The moment I turned from closing the door, Avi was beside me, smirking. "Looks like that's one test passed."

"Not entirely. Stay here for a sec." I trotted into the yard and stopped next to the magnolia tree. I beckoned to Avi. "Join me here?"

Avi's smirk vanished, and if he weren't a ghost, I'd say he looked constipated. Then he shook his head, walked down the steps, and crossed the grass to me, his feet mostly in contact with the ground.

"Maybe it's a sightline thing," he said. "If I can see you, I have to traverse the distance. If you're out of sight, I can just *be* there."

"Hmmm. I think we can explore that a little more later. Now, onward." I pointed toward Sofia's garden. "I'll walk that way slowly, aiming for that first row of tomato plants. You stay here as long as you can."

"All right."

I paced forward, counting steps and seconds, but when I'd passed our property line and was halfway to the garden, I glanced up at the scarecrow and winced. Since Carson was responsible for Avi's death—and hadn't been appropriately punished for it, in my opinion—Avi might not be comfortable keeping company with Carson-in-effigy. I turned back to where he was standing at the foot of the porch steps, about thirty feet away.

"Feel anything yet?"

"Maybe a twinge?"

"I should, um, mention something before you get any closer to the garden."

Avi's expression turned serious. "If it's because that's where Sofia collapsed—"

"No." I swallowed. That would probably affect me more than Avi. In fact, it *was* affecting me, if my cold hands were any indicator. I was just pretending to ignore it. "It's... You've seen the scarecrow from above, right?"

"Yes." He drew out that word in his typical fashion. "So?"

"It's... Well, it looks like Carson. I don't know if you—" Avi's laugh cut me off, and I scowled. "What's so funny?"

"You think the scarecrow is Carson?" Avi could barely get the words out.

I scowled, because this level of hilarity was hardly a proportional response. "Yes. It has the same hair. The same clothes. The face shape is a little different, but then, it's straw-stuffed burlap."

"The scarecrow isn't supposed to be *Carson*," he wheezed. "It's *Liam*."

I blinked at that. "Liam? Really?" Come to think of it, the later photos of Liam in Sofia's house—the ones where he was a blond—did bear a striking resemblance to the scarecrow. The face shape was definitely right. "Do you mean he and Carson actually *dressed* alike?" I couldn't keep the revulsion out of my tone.

"Oh my god, it was practically a *uniform* for them." Avi took off his glasses and wiped his eyes with a palm. "I'm not sure either of them even owned a pair of jeans or a single graphic T-shirt. For them, it was all about designer labels and name brand logos. I think they liked to pretend they were at an elite private school so they could look down on the other kids."

"Figures." I gestured toward the garage. "I'm heading over there to grab the hose. Give a holler when you feel like you're about to poof."

Instead of *heading* over, I backed away, keeping a close watch on Avi's expression for any sign of discomfort. When I reached the far edge of the garden, within five feet or so from the hose bib, Avi suddenly vanished.

"Well, crap," I muttered.

An instant later, he was beside me, a rueful expression on his face. "The sensation doesn't graduate. One moment I feel a twinge and a tug, and then I'm back in the house."

"That still gives us good information." I squinted at the property line where he'd been standing. "How far would you say that is?"

He rolled his eyes. "I was a writer. Oren's the one with spatial awareness. He could judge distances within an inch."

I cut a glance at Avi. He was looking back across the yard too, just as I'd been, and this was the first time I'd heard him make a comment about Oren that sounded almost absent and not as though he was trying to hold his heart inside his chest.

It occurred to me that getting out of the house, engaging in other activities, investigating his own abilities, might be more necessary for Avi's well-being than I'd considered. At home, he had nothing to distract himself from his grief.

Not that I imagined he'd get over Oren's loss any time soon, if ever, but I made a vow to myself to involve Avi in more... what? Enrichment activities? The house caged him in a way, and though he wasn't an infant by any means, he was still learning about himself and his world, much like a baby would.

I hoped the EVP equipment would arrive on schedule, because giving Avi the tools to make choices about his new reality had just shot to the top of my to-do list, and my reasons for making him my unofficial assistant at the Manor changed, too.

While helping Ghost-with-a-capital-G was important, it was no longer my top priority. My top priority was helping the ghost-with-a-lower-case-g.

My top priority was helping my friend.   .

CHAPTER FIFTEEN

Sofia's yellow and green striped garden hose was loaded onto one of those automatic retracting drums and had an industrial strength gun-type nozzle. All respect to Ricky for making the watering process both sturdy and efficient. I unrolled enough of it to reach the garden, but just as I pressed the trigger, I got distracted by the glint of silver on Birch Street. Consequently, I doused my shirt instead of the cucumbers.

"Crap!"

Avi snickered. "I'd offer to help, Maz, but I haven't unlocked my quick-dry function yet."

"Very funny," I muttered as I set the hose down, my soaked T-shirt clinging clammily to my skin. The sun wasn't up high enough to offer any warmth, but that didn't seem like an excuse for the shiver that ran from my nape to my tailbone. "This is what I get for making an early start."

"What happened? Does the hose have a leak?"

"No. I just have lousy aim." And I thought I saw something that should be impossible. Yeah, it *should* be impossible, but, you know, trust but verify. "Gotta check on something."

I hurried down Sofia's side yard with its long bed of perennial herbs, then stopped before I cleared the wall to peer around the corner.

Now I knew the shiver had nothing to do with my alfresco cold shower, because a silver Porsche was drawing up to the curb in front of my house in exactly the same spot it had parked a month ago.

"How can he be out of jail already?" I muttered. "And how can he possibly have his car?" Taryn had told me that Carson would have to liquidate his assets to pay the fines and damages for copyright infringement, let alone the fines for threatening me with a gun. Had he found some way to protect some of them from seizure?

"What is it?" When Avi spoke from behind me, I stumbled back a step. I'd worried about Avi's reaction to the scarecrow when I thought it was modeled on Carson. Seeing Carson in the flesh? I wouldn't subject him to that kind of trauma.

I turned to face him. "I think you should go back to the house."

"Why?"

"Um... because?"

Avi rolled his eyes. "You're a ghostwriter, Maz. Surely you can manufacture a more convincing reason than that."

"That's different." I waggled my fingers. "Words flow better through my hands than out of my mouth." I leaned backward until I could see the street and, sure enough, the driver's door opened and a blond head emerged. I ducked back. "I really think you should go back inside."

"I know I don't have much agency these days, but we're friends, and you're clearly unnerved by something. If I can help, I will. Whatever it is—"

"It's Carson," I blurted.

Even though Avi's skin was semi-transparent, I swore he paled. "Carson's here? How?"

"I don't know. But his car just pulled up in front of my house. I'll go see what he wants, but I don't want you to have to face him."

Avi's jaw tightened and his expression morphed into positively murderous. "Are you kidding? Maybe all I need to channel my poltergeist powers is a chance at that guy's face." He brushed past me, his stride longer than I'd ever seen.

"Avi. Wait."

Much to my shock, he did. He froze just beyond Sofia's porch, and the tension in his shoulders seemed to drain away. He turned and beckoned to me. "Come here, Maz."

"What?" I croaked. "Why? I don't want to see that guy either."

"It's not Carson. Take a look."

I peered around the corner at the man standing at the Porsche's rear bumper, fussing with something in his hand that I couldn't quite make out.

"Is that—"

"Yes," Avi said. "Once again, you've mistaken Liam for his evil twin, although this version is full of hot air instead of straw."

"For Pete's sake," I grumbled. "What's he doing with Carson's car?"

Avi squinted at Liam. "I don't think—"

"I hope he hasn't talked Sofia into buying it for him."

"That sounds like the kind of thing he would do, but—"

"Fine. I suppose I should meet him for Sofia's sake, anyway." I glanced down at my T-shirt. "I'll probably make just as good an impression on him as I did on Carson."

Nevertheless, I squared my shoulders and marched around the porch. Yeah, there was no doubt this man was the scarecrow's original source model. Hair, clothes, and, yes, the precise face shape. Ricky's cousin had *skills*.

Liam must have noticed my approach, because he looked up at me and his eyes widened. He stumbled back a step. "Don't come any closer. Stay back or I'll call the police."

Crap. I should probably slow my roll. I stopped and raised my hands, palms out, the gesture all too reminiscent of my first meeting with Carson. The threats of police involvement were the same too, but Carson had been all bravado and aggressive confidence. Liam just looked terrified.

"Sorry. Didn't mean to frighten you. I'm Maz."

To Liam's credit, he recovered his composure quickly. He tugged at the collar of his ice-blue button-down and managed to look down his nose at me, his mouth pinched with obvious disdain. "You should move along. We aren't looking to hire anybody for yard maintenance."

"Oh, this is going to go well," Avi murmured. "He's never going to forgive you for seeing his fear."

"You're not helping," I murmured out of the corner of my mouth.

Liam's eyes narrowed. "What did you say?"

"Once again, sorry. I think there's been a misunderstanding. I'm Maz Amani." I pointed at my house. "I live there."

I'd expected Liam's attitude to improve with the news that I wasn't some random guy trolling for work in a wet T-shirt at seven in the morning, but instead he added a layer of disapproval to his disdain.

"Maz? You're the one who got Avi's house."

He made it sound as though I'd snatched it out from under somebody's nose at a Black Friday sale at the mall. "I inherited it from my uncle—"

"Third cousin," Avi murmured, amusement clear in his tone. He was *enjoying* this, and it occurred to me that this was the first time in a while that he was speaking to me in the presence of somebody who didn't know about him.

Well, I'd let him have his fun. I didn't especially care about Liam's opinion of me, because it couldn't possibly be lower than my opinion of him.

He folded his arms. "Don't you think it would have been more appropriate for the house to go to family?"

I met his gaze. "It did."

"I mean Avi's family."

"It did," Avi growled. "Oren was my family."

"Regardless of your thoughts on the matter"—my voice might have been a touch too loud, judging by Liam's flinch— "the house belongs to me."

He snorted. "I was prepared to give you the benefit of the doubt, but now that I see how little respect you have for family ties—"

"Benefit of the doubt for what?"

"For assuming you had the authority to arrange travel plans for my grandmother."

I tried to give *him* the benefit of the doubt, keeping my voice level. "I'm not making any decisions for her, if that's what you're afraid of."

"What I'm afraid of is that she's not a well woman, and with your impulsive disregard for her health, you could well be the cause of her death. I could sue."

My jaw sagged. "I'm sorry. What?"

"For hospital bills. Funeral expenses. Physical and emotional distress."

Heat built in my throat and behind my eyes. "In the first place, Sofia is not dead."

He snorted again. "Not yet."

"You're not either," Avi growled, "but maybe something could be arranged."

For some reason, Avi's clear rage made it easier for me to dial back on my own. "Look. Kudos to you for making the effort to come see her so close to your graduation."

He blinked at that. "Yes. It was very inconvenient. Finals."

"I'm sure she'll be thrilled to see you, but from what I've heard so far, she's in no danger."

"Regardless, I'm the only person who should be making decisions for her."

"I'm pretty sure she's capable of making her own decisions."

He glanced up at the house. "That's debatable, considering she's living alone in a house that's entirely too big for her to manage at her age. If she could regulate her own medications, she wouldn't be in this situation."

"I don't think—"

"Maz!" With that shout to announce her, Ricky's sister Felicia leaped off the curb at the corner of Iris Lane and Main Street and flew toward us, her long black hair fanning behind her like a shining banner.

I waved. "Hey, Felicia."

As she reached our side of the street, she slowed down. "What happened to you?

"Oh. You mean this?" I pinched the wet shirt and pulled it away from my chest. Mistake, since when I let go, the fabric remained bunched like I'd sprouted a weird third nipple. "Ricky asked me to water Sofia's garden this morning, and I had a slight mishap with the hose."

Her laugh faded as her gaze flicked between me and Liam. "Guillermo? Is that you?"

Liam frowned, and Avi... disappeared.

Knowing how affectionate Ricky's family normally was with one another, I was surprised when Felicia hugged *me*, despite my soggy condition, and then simply turned to study Liam.

His frown deepened. "My name is Liam."

She winced. "Sorry. Last time you were here, I was just a kid and Tia still calls you Guillermo. I'll remember for next time, I promise. Did Ricky contact you?"

Liam seemed momentarily stunned by Felicia's shotgun approach to conversation. It took him a moment before he said, "Yes. That's right."

"She's not home from the hospital yet. I came by to get her car so I could do some grocery shopping since I'll be staying with her while she recovers. Are you going to the hospital now? I can take you. Oh!" She pointed at the Porsche. "You have your own ride, I see."

"I'm here to pick up a few things for Sofia," he said, his tone dripping with disapproval.

"Really?" Felicia cocked her head. "What?"

"Personal things she might need. Her purse. Her checkbook."

Felicia waved his words away. "No need. Mami stopped by last night and collected all that. Do you know where the hospital is in Richdale? Oh! I forgot. You grew up there mostly, didn't you?" She laughed a little. "You probably know the place better than I do. If you hurry, you can get there when visitor's hours start."

I wasn't aware that Liam's frown could deepen, but clearly I had underestimated his abilities. "She's allowed visitors?"

"Eh." Felicia waggled her hand. "We're allowed. Antonio— you remember Antonio, don't you? Uncle Federico's middle son? He's the charge nurse on her floor."

Wow. If there were a frown Olympics, Liam would snag the gold without breaking a sweat. "That's incredibly irresponsible of him and inconsiderate of all of you. Think of Sofia. You're endangering her recovery. It could be months—"

"Oh, no. Not months. In fact, she should be home by Sunday." Felicia's smile was brilliant. "She's decided on the ablation procedure."

"What?" Liam seemed sincerely shocked. "Surgery? She can't — The risks are too great."

"They're not, really," I said. "Not any more than letting the SVT worsen."

He turned his gold-medal scowl on me. "What would you know about it?"

"My grandmother had the same condition. She opted for the ablation when she was in her sixties and kicked herself for not doing it years earlier."

"See?" Felicia looped her arm through my elbow. "She'll be ready to travel by the end of the month, so when we're there for your graduation, she won't even be on meds anymore. Isn't that great?"

"No, it is not great." Liam's chest heaved like a bellows, nostrils flaring in a way that was reminiscent of Greg—or a bull about to charge. "I see that I need to have a serious talk with

Sofia, because clearly the rest of you are thinking only of your own enjoyment and not her well-being. And *you*."

He thrust his hand at me, index finger fairly vibrating, and the gold charm on his key chain nearly bonked me on the nose. I went nearly cross-eyed staring at it, but I refused to back away. Pretty ballsy of Liam to spend Sofia's money on a Massachusetts keychain in what looked like solid gold, although whoever crafted it hadn't quite gotten the shape right. My geography app project would probably have tagged it as a coffee pot.

"What about me?"

"While your gesture was no doubt well-intentioned, I trust you'll see now that it was extremely ill-judged and take appropriate action."

He turned and strode toward the Porsche, brushing past three people who had stopped on the sidewalk in front of my house.

"Well," I said. "He seems nice."

CHAPTER SIXTEEN

As Felicia and I watched Liam drive away, somebody cleared their throat.

"Is this a bad time?"

I realized that the people Liam had barreled past on his way to Carson's car—a woman with silvering blond hair, a man, also blond, but without the silver, who was probably a decade or so younger, and a pre-teen girl whose round face and wide blue eyes indicated a relationship to both adults, even though her hair was dark brown and curly—were still standing on the sidewalk, all smiling tentatively at us. The woman was the one who had spoken.

I sighed. "That depends, I suppose." I forced a smile. "What can I do for you?"

"Hi!" The girl waved enthusiastically. "I'm Jillie Vlahos and this is my mom, Bernadette, and my uncle, Dominik." She blinked up at me. "Could we please, please, *please* see your house?"

"My house?" I glanced up the walk at the porch. "Why? If somebody told you it's for sale, they've misled you."

"Jillie." Bernadette looked down at her daughter. "Don't you think we should tell him who we are first?"

Jillie's brows knotted in obvious confusion. "I just did."

"You told him our *names*."

"Yes." She glanced between Bernadette and me, clearly confused.

"So why would he know them?"

"But... but this is a small town. Everyone always knows everything about everybody else."

Dominik chuckled and tugged a lock of Jillie's hair. "That's only true on those shows you watch." He turned his smile on me, and although his dimples were cute, he didn't pack near Ricky's wattage. "She's a big fan of Hallmark movies." He held out his hand. "We're the new owners of Jenkins House. Bernadette's handling the food and I'll be managing the place."

"Jenkins House? Oh! The B & B." I shook his hand. "You must be who Taryn was meeting with on Wednesday. Taking over from your aunt and uncle, right?"

Jillie gestured to me with both hands. "See? Everyone knows *everything*."

I laughed and shook Bernadette's hand too. "Not quite. Taryn's one of my closest friends, and she was on her way to meet you when I last saw her. She didn't tell me your names, only that the place was changing hands. She's really not in the habit of disclosing her clients' personal information. I'm Maz Amani." I winked at Jillie. "But you probably already knew that."

Felicia thrust her hand out. "And I'm Felicia Vargas."

"Vargas?" Bernadette's gaze sharpened. "Of Taqueria Vargas?"

Felicia nodded as she made the rounds of handshakes. "My family owns it, yes."

"Are you related to Sofia Vargas, then?" Dominik asked.

"She's my aunt."

"Well, *our* aunt told us that *your* aunt's tres leches cake is something special, and that Bernadette needs to beg a lesson from her. Could you introduce us?"

Felicia shared a glance with me. "I— I'd be glad to, and I'm sure she'd be happy to give you some tips, but she's not at home right now. Maybe next week?"

Dominik nodded affably. "No hurry. We've got some work to do before we open. Figure out how to make the place our own, you know?"

"Why did you want to see my house?" I asked.

Since Jillie was staring at the house, her mouth slightly open and her eyes wide, Bernadette answered. "Because of Oren Buckley, of course. He did such beautiful work on Jenkins House that when we found out he lived here, we really wanted to see it."

At that moment, I was glad that Avi had bugged out on me. As much as I'd have appreciated his commentary on Liam's attitude, I doubted he was quite ready to hear strangers flinging Oren's name around, talking about him *living here* when he'd never had a chance to move in.

"I'd be happy to arrange that, but"—I gestured to my shirt—"I'm a little too damp for comfort right now, and I need to head to work shortly. Maybe tonight?"

"Maz." Felicia tugged on my T-shirt hem. "I forgot to tell you that Ricky was hoping you'd have dinner with him tonight."

I blinked. "He was? He didn't text me."

She huffed. "Okay, fine. Mami and Papi and I were hoping you'd have dinner with him. We figured you were the only person who stood half a chance of dragging him away from Tia."

"I, um, can do that." I had my dad's cookbooks again. Maybe I could make him something, provided I had time after work.

Felicia clapped. "Bueno! You've got his truck keys, right?" I nodded. "Also bueno." She leaned toward the Vlahoses and stage-whispered, "My brother afraid to ride in Maz's car because it's such a piece of—"

"Hey! Don't tell me you're trying to talk me into buying a new car, too. What, does your cousin cut you in on the commission or give you a finder's fee or something?"

She patted my shoulder. "No, Maz. We all just want you to be safe. Take the truck, okay?"

"Fine," I grumbled.

"I've got to run." She waved at the Vlahoses. "It was great to meet you. Be sure to stop in the Taqueria sometime soon, okay?" She jogged off across the lawn, then turned, although she continued moving, jogging backward. "Maz, could you come around and close the garage door for me? Tia doesn't have an automatic opener, and I'm already running late for school."

"No problem."

When I turned back to the Vlahoses, Jillie's eyes were even wider. "Is Ricky your *boyfriend*?" she whispered.

I pointed at her forehead. "Despite what you think you know about small towns, you're not entitled to poke that into everything."

She flushed nearly scarlet. "Sorry." She heaved a sigh. "And I'm not totally clueless. I know small towns can't *really* be like they are in movies, otherwise this one would be haunted, right?"

It was my turn to blink. "Uh..."

"Although I guess that would be a little too *obvious* and.... and..." She looked up at her uncle. "What did you call it, Uncle Dom?"

"On the nose," he replied.

"Yeah!" She turned back to me. "Too on the nose for a place called Ghost."

"Yes. Absolutely. One hundred percent." I cleared my throat. "How about this? Why don't you three come over for dinner tomorrow? We can get to know one another in a more *organic* way. I'll get takeout from the Taqueria."

"What if..." Bernadette bit her lip. "That is, may I cook for you? For you *and* Ricky?"

Dominik nodded. "That's the best way for you to get to know us. Bernadette can mutter to her food—"

"I do not *mutter*." Bernadette turned almost as pink as Jillie. "I *commune*. It's my *process*."

"And," Dominik continued as though she hadn't spoken although he had a definite twinkle in his eye, "I can chat with you and Ricky in between Jillie trying to pump you for details on your house and the rest of the people in town." He glanced at his sister and niece. "We can hit Taqueria Vargas tonight."

"Sounds like a plan," I said while Jillie clapped and bounced on her toes. I turned to Bernadette. "What time do you need to start your prep?"

She waved a hand. "I'll do most of that at Jenkins House. For what I have in mind, I won't need much actual stove time."

"How about six?"

"Perfect. We'll see you then."

I stood under my maple tree, watching them walk away. Ghost's population was growing—first me, then the Vlahoses. At the corner of Main Street, Jillie turned and waved at me. I waved back, grinning. If my plan to get Avi to assist me with Thaddeus's effects panned out, the Vlahoses would have enough business to, well, keep themselves in business. Of course, if Bernadette was a terrible chef, that could be a problem. I guess I'd find out tomorrow.

I froze with my hand still in the air.

I'd just invited three strangers into the house I shared with Avi. We hadn't discussed how he felt about having unknown people in our space because, frankly, other than me, there weren't any unknown people around here.

Would it upset him? Send him back into his paper vortex phase? We still didn't know how his manifestation worked, what might set him off, or worse, what might block him from manifesting at all. What if the reason he could manifest was because everything in the house was familiar? He'd started to appear more often over the last month as we'd gotten to be…

Yes, he'd said it, and so had I. We were more than just housemates. We were friends. I suspected that Avi was even more of an introvert than I was, and introverted friends didn't blindside their other introverted friends with unexpected dinner parties.

Ugh. Surprises. I hated them. If Avi hated them as much as I did, he wouldn't be happy.

I frowned, patting my pocket as I trudged up the porch steps. The ring was still there, but Avi hadn't returned after the Vlahoses had arrived. That might give me my answer right there.

I sighed and slipped in the front door. Gil wasn't lurking in the vestibule in an attempt to dart outside. He could just be off napping somewhere or plotting his next stealth attack on some innocent, unsuspecting knickknack, but I hoped it meant he was with Avi.

"Avi?" I called. "You around?"

At first there was no response, but then I heard a soft, "In the library."

When I walked through the french doors, I didn't spot him at first. He was sitting on the window seat, gazing out into the yard, with Gil purring next to him, but he was even more see-through than usual.

"Hey." I stopped next to the desk. "I think I owe you an apology."

He looked up at me. "Why?"

"I just invited three strangers to dinner."

"Three str— You mean those people you were talking to just now?"

"Yes. Bernadette, Dominik, and Jillie Vlahos. Bernadette's a chef. She's going to cook here tomorrow. At six."

Avi's pensive expression relaxed into a smile. "Maz, you don't need to get permission from me to invite people to your house."

"*Our* house. It's only polite. Especially with these people."

He cocked his head. "Why them in particular?"

"They're the new owners of Jenkins House. They, um, want to see this place because Oren remodeled it, too."

"Oh." He turned away, his throat working. "I'd… like to see Jenkins House again. Do you think…" He looked up at me, his expression hopeful. "Do you think they'd give you a reciprocal tour sometime? And you could bring me with you?"

"Of course." I sat on the opposite curve of the window seat. "They seem really nice, so I'm sure they'd agree. You're sure you're not upset? When you didn't come back outside earlier—"

"It wasn't them," he said hurriedly. "To be honest, I hadn't even noticed them. It was Felicia."

"Felicia?"

He rubbed the back of his neck, not meeting my gaze. "There's something about standing right next to somebody I used to know and having them look right through me." He chuckled. "Not that people didn't look right through me before." He cut a quick glance at my face. "Almost everybody except—"

"Except Oren."

He nodded. "And now you." He rubbed his chest, right over his heart. "I don't think it hit me before how long I've been… gone. Everyone I've seen here at the house so far were adults when I was alive. Once you hit that benchmark, inhabiting your… your mature container, I guess, and you don't have the artificial yardstick of school years, you kind of assume everyone's your age. But Felicia… The last time I saw her, she was about four feet tall, wore her hair in pigtails but had recently given herself an unfortunate crooked fringe, and was missing both front teeth." He took a breath. "It was a definite wake-up call. Despite everything we've been through in the last month, I don't think I really believed it until now."

"I get it. You don't have to ever apologize to me for taking time to process things." I pulled one leg up to my chest and rested my chin on my kneecap. "I'm a little envious that you're able to exit uncomfortable situations so effortlessly. No awkward goodbyes or lies about getting in touch later. You can just *go* and nobody will be any the wiser. I can't tell you how many times I wished for that kind of instant escape."

"I don't recommend my method of achieving it," he said dryly.

I grimaced. "Sorry."

"It's all right."

"It's not." I really wished I could grip his shoulders, but I settled for locking my gaze with his. "We may not have all the answers about your situation, but *you* are the one who gets to decide what's right for you, and that includes other clueless people"—I jerked both thumbs toward my chest—"making thoughtless comments or stupid jokes at your expense. So if I do it and I don't catch myself? Call me on it, okay?"

He drew his lower lip between his teeth for a moment, then nodded. "Okay."

"Good. Now. I need to change into drier clothes and water the garden." I paused, remembering my less than successful interactions with the garden hose. "Strike that. Reverse it. Garden first, then dry clothes, and *then* we can head for the Manor."

He angled his head, a smile quirking the corner of his mouth. "Can't wait for the first official Take Your Ghost to Work Day?"

I held my hands up. "Hey, you said it, not me."

CHAPTER SEVENTEEN

After closing the butler's pantry door to keep a very disgruntled Gil from following us into the mudroom, I tossed my keys up and grabbed them out of the air. Jingling them in my hand, I grinned at Avi as we crossed to the garage.

I grabbed the doorknob. "Ready?"

"Will you stop that?" he said irritably.

"Stop what?"

"Rattling your keys."

"Sorry. Nervous energy." I tucked the key ring in my hoodie pocket, opened the door, and gestured for Avi to precede me. "After you."

He didn't move. "Are you sure about this? Remember the laptop bluescreen incident?"

"My car predates modern computer controls, so as long as you don't get too close to the battery or the ignition, I think we'll be okay. There's not much more you could fritz out in there. The radio's already busted, and so are the dome lights, so... so..."

Avi peered at me. "What? You've got that look."

"What look? I have a look?"

"Don't hedge. That look you get when you retrieve some obscure fact from your vast store of ghostwriting minutia and make a mental connection. A lightbulb moment."

I chuckled weakly. "A lightbulb moment. That's appropriate."

"Maz. Stop stalling. What just occurred to you?"

"Well." I flipped the switch to turn on the brushed steel wall sconces that flanked the door. "Lights."

"Lights?"

"Yes. Lights. I mean, think about it. There are light fixtures all over the house and you've never blown them out. The typewriter, too. You used it when it wasn't turned on." Heck, it might not have even been plugged in for all I remembered. I'd been a little distracted at the time because my new house had been vandalized and I'd slept through the whole thing.

"So?"

"So I was assuming that because of the laptop bluescreen incident—"

He winced. "I said I was sorry about that."

"I know. No worries. It recovered."

I descended onto the garage's single concrete step and motioned for him to join me. He hesitated, wringing his hands in his signature anxiety tell, but finally followed. I realized that while we were both nervous about the potential of his visit to the Manor, we saw it from completely different perspectives.

For me, it was like a door opening on new information that could change everything, for Avi and for Ghost. But for Avi, it was the opposite possibility—a door closing in his face, its dead bolts thrown and key lost forever. Proof that he had nothing more to hope for.

"Hey," I said softly. "You okay?"

Once again, he hesitated. Then he squared his shoulders and nodded, a muscle ticking in his jaw. "I'll be fine. Go on."

I waited a moment, but he had the air of determination that I'd come to recognize.

"I think we—or at least *I*—made an assumption that might not be correct."

He canted an eyebrow. "Really, Maz? An assumption? You?"

If Avi could dial up his snark again, I figured we were good to go.

"Shocking, I know. I assumed that your presence interfered with electronics and, by extension, electrical things. But I don't think that could be correct. The wi-fi router works, and one of the nodes is in the attic. You walk past it, and all the other nodes, all the time. Maybe it has more to do with... I don't know... circuit interruption? Like there's a critical instant"—I jerked my chin at the car—"like a point of ignition or the moment the current connects to a lamp or a toaster that you *could* interrupt if you touched it at the right time."

This time, Avi got a look—I'd seen it before, whenever he was tracing a memory or evaluating a problem. His eyebrows lowered behind the rim of his glasses, his head tilted slightly, and his eyes seemed to focus on the distance.

"I suppose," he said slowly.

If I was right, it would mean two major breakthroughs about Avi's abilities in as many days. I gripped the keys in my pocket and nearly pulled them out to toss in my palm again, but resisted in consideration of Avi's nerves.

"Think about it. That time the laptop bluescreened, you'd pointed to something in the document I was working on. Your finger was close to the screen, but nothing happened. Everything was fine. But when you leaned your hand on the table, you misjudged the distance and your fingers passed through the keyboard."

"Sorry." He glanced away, clearly embarrassed. "My spatial awareness sucks."

"It'll get better. You're just not used to being a ghost yet."

"It has nothing to do with being a ghost." He turned a glare on me. "My spatial awareness has *always* sucked."

"My *point*—and I do have one—is that computer circuits pass signals around constantly. There's more traffic happening, so there's more opportunity to interrupt one of those signals than, say, preventing a single connection when a light switch gets flipped or a key turns in the ignition."

He lifted an eyebrow and gestured toward the Civic. "Are you volunteering your car as a test case?"

"And risk being wrong?" I shook my head. "Not a chance. That would feed right in to the campaign to get me to buy a new car."

"Oooh. We should *definitely* try it out then." Avi grinned and waggled his fingers. "Just a little touch to interrupt the signal, you said? I may need a few tries to get the timing right."

As much as I didn't want to fry my car's ignition, I was so happy to see Avi's playful mood that I nearly agreed to let him give it a go. But we had something more important on the agenda today. "Let's make our first forays into circuit interruption on something less expensive and immediately necessary than my car, okay? We've got the whole Manor waiting for us."

He wrinkled his nose. "A roomful of dusty papers. Oh, joy."

"A roomful of dusty papers that could give us clues about how the whole ghost thing works."

"A point. All right." He studied the Civic. "How do you suggest I enter?"

"Uh...through the door."

"Which I can't open."

"That didn't seem to stop you on the porch earlier."

"Because you were on the other side with the ring."

I spread my arms as though encompassing the house beyond the garage. "But we're still within your domain. You've always moved through the house."

"Yes, but not *inside* something that isn't part of the house." He cast a revolted glance at the car. "And that is definitely *not* a part of the house, nor would I ever want it to be."

"This is a good trial, then." I leaned against the wall. "See if you can get in on your own. If you can't, I'll climb behind the wheel and you should be able to join me."

He shot me a skeptical glance. "On your head be it."

His shoulders rose and fell once, twice, three times, and then he marched over to the passenger door, his feet mostly touching the concrete floor. He frowned, staring down at the handle before shaking his head and reaching toward the window—and then *through* the window.

"Come on, come on," I murmured, practically bouncing on my toes. "You can do it."

Avi pulled his hand back, frown deepening, and took a step forward until he was standing partway through the door.

He stepped back, shaking both hands. "That feels… weird."

"Weird bad or just weird?"

"I don't know. Although I'm not anxious to try it again. It's like…" He gazed up at the ceiling, gnawing on his lower lip, and sketched an unidentifiable shape in the air with both hands. "I'm not acquainted with it, or at least I wasn't when I was alive. It's present here"—he glanced at me sidelong—"but from the perspective of my *domain*, it doesn't *belong* here, so I can't interact with it in an ordinary way."

"Like sitting in the passenger seat?"

"Yes. Exactly."

I held up my keys while patting my pocket that held Oren's ring. "Then I guess we'll try it the other way."

I wrestled the driver's door open and got in. Before I could wrench the door closed with its usual metallic protest, Avi was sitting in the seat next to me.

"That was quick." I punched the garage door opener on my visor and started the engine, which only sputtered once or twice before it caught.

He just shrugged. "I guess I needed the ring's presence to induct the car into the *domain*."

"That term really bothers you, doesn't it?"

"It reeks of toxic privilege."

After the door trundled up, I backed the car out, making sure the door rolled down behind us before I headed down the short drive and onto Iris Lane. "Really? To me, it reeks of medieval cosplay or internet branding and annual payments to a web host, but whatever."

"Mmm."

Even without his noncommittal reply, I could tell he wasn't paying attention to me. Instead, he was leaning forward, gazing avidly through the windows as Main Street unrolled in front of us.

Now, don't get me wrong, Ghost's Main Street is totally charming, but Avi was looking at it as if... as if...

As if he hadn't seen it in more than ten years.

I kept any snarky judgmental comments locked behind my teeth and let up on the gas, slowing down to fifteen miles an hour. Yes, it was ten MPH slower than the limit, and if my dad had been driving behind me, he'd be turning the air blue, but there was no traffic this morning, so I wasn't inconveniencing anybody.

And even if I was? I didn't really care. Avi's experience was more important.

"You okay?" I asked.

Avi took a shaky breath, his hands clutching his knees. "It's lighting up so many memories." He gestured toward the window. "Now that I see it, I can tell that a couple of stores are missing. One restaurant. And the knitting shop and occult supply are merged. But it looks... cared for. Not derelict at all."

"I'm pretty sure that the Ghost townies wouldn't allow that to happen. They love this town and they're all really proud of it."

He glanced at me with a crooked smile. "Don't you mean *we* love this town and *we're* really proud of it?"

I laughed softly. "Yeah. Yeah, I guess I do."

An awkward silence descended as I turned onto Violet Road and drove along the Manor's fence. To break it, I asked, "Did you visit the Manor much when you were a kid?"

He nodded. "It was a regular school field trip for third and sixth graders before they closed the elementary school and shipped everyone to Richdale. Ricky and Taryn and their age group got the third grade trip, but not the sixth."

"Did you visit outside those trips?"

"I worked there as a junior docent for a little while when I was a high school sophomore, but even then, tourism had started to drop off, so my summer job ended up being only two days a week and ended in the middle of August." He shrugged. "After that? I don't think I ever went back." He snorted. "I probably thought I knew everything there was to know about the place, so why bother? It's not as though there were any actual *ghosts* there."

"Teenage disdain. It's a hard bar to clear." I slowed as we neared the main entrance, where the *Closed* sign was still posted inside the open gates. "But that'll change today. Because as of today, there *will* be an actual ghost there." I pulled into the drive, easing over the speed bump between gateposts.

"I guess you're right. I wonder if—" Avi gasped and leaned back until he was halfway inside the seat. "Maz. Stop. Stop the car. Stop!"

I slammed on the brakes, glad that there was nobody behind me. "What is it?"

"I... I can't. I have to leave. Now."

I threw the car into reverse and backed up. Once we were clear of the grounds, Avi let out a shaky breath and bent nearly double, his arms wrapped across his stomach.

"Avi? What's wrong? Are you okay? Does something about the Manor frighten you?"

"It doesn't frighten me." He turned his head to peer up at me and I recoiled, bonking my head against the window. I'd never seen that look on Avi's face before, not even when he'd found out what Carson had done to him.

Pure, unadulterated rage.

"If I go through those gates, Maz, I don't know what I'll do."

"What? Why?"

He shook his head, his cardigan bunched in his clenched fists. "Something in there is pissing me off for no reason at all. It's... It's fraying my control, nipping at the edge of my consciousness. I have to go home before I do something I'll regret. Before I hurt somebody. Before I hurt *you*."

"Okay. Okay. It's fine." When I'd spoken to Marguerite Windflower—aka Peg—she'd told me that Thaddeus Richdale had done something that actively repelled spirits. I didn't think it would *enrage* them, or that it could still be in effect. "I'll drive you back."

He choked on a laugh. "You don't have to drive me, Maz. Getting home is never a problem. I'll see you tonight."

"I, um, have a date to pick Ricky up tonight."

"Then I guess I'll see you both." He took another deep breath. "Don't worry about me. I'll be fine."

Then he was gone.

"Well, crap." I put the car in Drive and passed through the gates again. "And like hell will I not worry about you, Avi."

I now had a new goal. Somewhere in the piles of Richdale family detritus, there had to be a clue about what Thaddeus had done to drive ghosts away. I'd find it, and once I did, I'd rip it out by its roots.

Avi didn't deserve to live right across the freaking road from something that threatened him like this. Also, if this mysterious whatever-it-was was keeping other ghosts away, then it definitely had to go, not only for the sake of the town, but again for Avi.

Because if there wasn't some supernatural blockage in place preventing it, there was one spirit who'd do everything in his phantasmagorical power to get back to Ghost, and it wasn't Thaddeus or Jonah Richdale.

It was Oren Buckley.

CHAPTER EIGHTEEN

My car was the only one in the lot, so the rest of the staff must have taken advantage of Saul's offer of an extra day off after the event. However, I had a key to the side door that led to the hallway with the servants' staircase that Saul and I always used to get up to the second floor. His office and the document room where I worked weren't on the regular tour path. We never heard any commotion from the gift shop or ran into parties as they wandered through the Manor, so why did the place feel extra silent and deserted this morning?

Maybe because I didn't expect to be alone.

I practically crept down the passage to the document room, and once I was there, I couldn't focus. I wanted to find the thing —whatever it was—that was affecting Avi, but I didn't know where to start. As ashamed as I was to admit it, I'd never taken the official tour of the Manor, and I couldn't remedy that fact today.

It didn't feel right to poke around the place on my own. I doubt Saul would have objected if I'd asked, but I hadn't asked, so that option was off the table. I couldn't even reference Frances Richdale's journal because Saul had sent it to a bookbinder to have it professionally disassembled, the pages photographed in high resolution, and then rebound so we could sell hardcover facsimiles in the Manor gift shop and an ebook version online.

I'd been surprised about the digital option.

"We have an online store?" I'd asked Saul.

E.J. Russell

"We do. Mostly for ticket sales and tour reservations." He sighed. "I've always intended to do more with it, but somehow all my time gets taken up with fundraising, so..." He spread his hands in a *what-can-you-do* gesture. Then his lips curled up in a smile and his brown eyes sparkled. "I don't suppose you'd consider adding internet content creation to your document sorting tasks. I could ask Taryn to amend the contract to account for it."

I waved that away. "The contract is more than generous, and we'd talked about putting together a book about the family based on their papers, so I don't think this counts as scope creep."

Saul had been adamant. "Web content wasn't part of the original deal. I'll let Taryn know."

I'd promptly forgotten about it following Carson's arrest and discovering that Avi was Jake freaking Fields, my favorite thriller writer. Maybe now would be a good time to make a list of possible blog post topics. I rubbed the back of my neck, staring at the stacks of crates I hadn't even peeked in yet.

"There's certainly enough potential source material," I muttered. As a hoarder, Thaddeus Richdale was no slouch.

I closed my eyes, spun around twice, and, while I recovered my balance, flung out an arm, finger extended. When I opened my eyes, I was pointing at a battered cardboard box partially hidden in a totally unnecessary and peculiarly shaped niche.

"All right, little box. You weren't even on my radar, but let's see what you've got to tell me."

I hauled it over to the table I used for sorting contents as I unpacked each container, coughing at the cloud of dust that puffed out when I set it down. I don't know what I was hoping for—maybe crumbling parchment with jagged letters in ink the color of dried blood that said *Beware the cursed monkey's paw!*

Hey, what can I say? It's a classic.

Unfortunately, that wasn't the case here. Instead, the box contained several lace collars wrapped in yellowed tissue paper

144

and half a dozen thin, oversized books in some kind of rough gray binding that was definitely not leather.

I set the collars aside carefully—Saul would probably be able to use them in one of the room displays—and lifted out the first book.

"Please be another journal, please be another journal."

My muttered plea to the universe wasn't exactly answered, but it wasn't exactly ignored either.

No, the book wasn't a journal, nor was it written by one of the Richdales. Instead, it was their housekeeper's ledger. And whoever their housekeeper had been, they were the spiritual ancestor of the company that packed up Oren's effects, because while they were lousy at categorization and logical grouping, they were fantastic at listing the detail for each item purchased.

I peered at the bottom of one page and noted the faded date accompanied by a flowing signature in sepia ink—Frances Richdale. I snorted.

"Frances Richdale, matriarch of corporate micromanagers everywhere."

In her journal, Frances had flat out stated that Thaddeus was wasting their financial resources on his quest to pierce the veil "to the great detriment of our Family's wealth and well-being." From the looks of this, she was either keeping her housekeeper honest or doing her best to control a budget that was bleeding heavily from the cash outflow caused by Thaddeus's inability to grasp the sunk-cost fallacy.

Because holy *crap*, some of this stuff was expensive, especially for that time period.

This could actually be a good topic for a blog post, maybe not the inaugural one, but close after the introduction—a list of the supplies Thaddeus used for his research. I peered at the page again, noting the large amount of garlic and excessive number of silver chains. *Or maybe the supplies Frances used to* interfere *with his research.*

Had *Frances* been the one to stumble upon the spirit-repelling artifact? According to her journals, she certainly hadn't been a fan, although her entries had been observations of Thaddeus's attempts, rather than plans for anything that would block them.

The housekeeper's ledger contained item descriptions, but not always the reason for the purchase. For example, *"Haunch of venison requested for Mr. Holum's dinner"* was pretty clear, especially since each page also included a list of who was staying at the Manor on that date. Mr. Broderick Holum of San Francisco evidently had a taste for venison and a hearty appetite.

However, it had nothing more to say about the *"carved purple chalcedony locket on golden chain"* or *"rings of braided Andalusian horsehair (5) wound with silver thread."* Maybe it figured those were self-explanatory?

What would anybody do with five rings of braided horsehair, anyway, Andalusian or not, regardless of what thread they had wrapped around them?

Victorian spiritualists could be super weird.

My chuckle died in my throat as I spotted the date next to Frances's signature—it was more than two years prior to the first entry in her journal.

While Frances's journal had been explicit about the *what* of Thaddeus's attempts—that is, what he was hoping to achieve with any given experiment—they hadn't been very specific about *how* he intended to accomplish it. Well, she'd described the activities, but not what the participants had used for them in anything but general terms. I remembered every seance called for *three white candles.*

But this page of the housekeeper's ledger had an entry for *beeswax candles, 12 inches, three dozen, scented with lavender, tinted black.*

Somewhere between this date and Frances's journal, Thaddeus had switched from black candles to white. Why?

Excitement began to crawl from my belly up through my chest. If I could match actual materials from the housekeeper's accounts to the journal's events, I'd be able to match Thaddeus's goal with what he'd used to reach it. If nothing else, it would tell us what *not* to try investigating regarding Avi's abilities.

And maybe, just *maybe*, if I was very lucky, I'd find that break in the timeline. Because I can't imagine that something that would result in repelling all spirits within a hundred-mile radius could possibly be a small thing.

I remembered how fascinated I'd been by the historian's research methods in *The Daughter of Time*, how he and the bedridden detective had used sources other than "official" history to build their case for absolving Richard III of murdering the princes in the tower.

History was too easily revised by the winners in any conflict, and people—even the most well-intentioned—had a tendency to cast themselves and their "team" in the best possible light. To get the real picture, you had to look at objective facts. Things that had no reason to be either sanctified or demonized. Frances, in her journal, had a clear bias—she thought Thaddeus was an idiot for pursuing his obsession to communicate with Josiah, and furthermore, she resented the hell out of him for wasting their family money to do it.

Frances's journal only covered about eighteen months, from September 1906 until March 1908, when Frances had been in her mid-thirties. She'd introduced the volume with a very telling paragraph:

Whereas my Husband has devoted all our Resources to his Pursuits, it behooves me to chronicle his Actions, ere he once again repeat failed Trials to no avail and to the great detriment of our Family's wealth and well-being.

From that, it was clear that Thaddeus's experiments had been going on for some time. I suspected—I hoped—that somewhere in all these boxes I'd find other volumes of her journal and I'd be able to align them with the housekeeper's ledgers.

My cell phone vibrated in my pocket. I wiped the dust off my hands and pulled it out, hoping for a text from Ricky.

It wasn't, but it was equally exciting in a completely different way: a delivery notification from UPS. My EVP equipment had been delivered and left on the porch.

I checked the time—eleven thirty. That was totally legit for an early lunch, right, especially on a day I wasn't required to be working? I grabbed my hoodie and hurried down to my car.

I laughed to myself as I drove out of the empty lot. Saul Pasternak was probably the least-demanding boss in the history of the world—witness what amounted to an extra paid holiday for Manor staff. However, if the EVP equipment worked as I hoped, he'd probably forgive me for anything short of burning down the Manor, because it would mean that he could speak with Avi. That *anyone* could speak with Avi.

More importantly, though, it would mean that *Avi* could speak to anybody *he* wanted.

When I got home, I didn't bother pulling into the garage. Instead, I just pulled into the driveway and ran to the front porch. The box wasn't sitting in front of the door, and my stomach plummeted. I didn't *think* there could be much package theft here in Ghost, but I hadn't expected murder, either, and I'd been wrong about that.

Then I spotted it tucked under the porch swing and gave the UPS driver props for the camouflage win. I unlocked the door first, then teased the box out and hefted it into my arms. It wasn't particularly heavy, but it was awkwardly bulky. Opening the door wide enough that I could maneuver inside without letting Gil escape might be a challenge.

He was lurking next to the stairs, so I deduced that Avi must not be manifesting anywhere. He made a break for it, but I butted the door closed with my, well, butt, and earned a displeased rumble from him.

"I don't know why you've suddenly developed this hankering for the great outdoors, big guy, but we need to have a serious talk about it." I headed for the kitchen with him slinking along at my heels, ears swiveled back and tail down. "And stop sulking. You may think the grass is greener out there... Okay, I suppose the grass *is* greener because there's actual grass, but birds aren't nearly as easy to catch as you seem to think." I plopped the box onto the counter and looked down at him. "They have wings, Gil. Wings. They're not just mice with feathers."

Gil's ears perked up, and he bounded back into the family room.

"Hello, gorgeous," Avi said.

"Don't encourage him," I called. "He tried to bust out again."

Avi walked into the kitchen with Gil trotting next to him. "Has he always done that?"

"Never. He's always been curious and *interested*, especially when birds were involved, so I was always careful not to tempt him. Made sure the doors were closed, that kind of thing. This prison break behavior didn't pop up until a couple of days ago." I spread my arms. "Granted, we've never lived anywhere that *out* was particularly enticing, but he's got more room to explore here than in any of our previous places, so I don't know what the deal is."

Avi bent down to pet Gil. "Maybe he's just lonely. Didn't you always work from home before?"

"Yeah." I hunkered down to skritch Gil's ears. "Do you think that's it?"

He shrugged. "Maybe. I can try to be around more." He rolled his eyes. "Assuming I can figure out how."

"Do you, er, manifest while I'm not here?"

Avi screwed his mouth to one side, clearly wracking his brain. "I'm not sure. When you're not around, there's not much I need to do, so maybe not?"

"When you left the car earlier, do you remember appearing somewhere specific in the house? Doing anything there?"

He grimaced. "No. I just walked down the stairs now because I heard you talking to Gil. Do you suppose I can't be present unless there's a reason?"

"I don't like to think so," I said, frowning. "That denotes lack of choice. You should have enough agency to be able to show up whenever you want."

"Ah." He held up one forefinger. "But what do I want? That's the question, isn't it?"

Unfortunately, we both knew the answer to that one. He wanted Oren. The company Gil and I had to offer was a poor substitute, but at least it was *something*.

I stood and laid my palm atop the box. "So when Ricky and I went to Portland the other day, I had an idea."

He raised both palms in mock horror. "Maz, as much as I appreciate your friendship, I do not want to hear about your awkward attempts to woo Ricky."

"And yet, you're the one who suggested I buy new clothes for that very purpose." I folded my arms. "Do you want to hear my idea or not?"

"I'm sorry. By all means, continue."

"Ricky and I stopped at a falafel place for lunch—"

"The one in the Pearl?"

I blinked. "You know it?"

"It was one of Oren's favorite spots. He took me there a couple of times when I visited him in the city. He said it had been recommended to him by his cousin's husb— Oh."

CHAPTER NINETEEN

A combination of anger and longing washed over me, thickening my throat, and I croaked, "By my dad."

Why, why, *why* hadn't Oren reached out to me? It would have meant so much to have someone who knew my folks and *liked* them. My mom had been estranged from most of her family for years, first because she'd married my dad and then because of me. Yeah, being related to a bunch of racist homophobes was really freaking awesome.

"I'm sorry, Maz."

"It's okay."

"No. It's not."

I sighed. "You're right. But there's absolutely nothing either of us can do about the past, so"—I gestured to the box—"moving on."

Avi studied the box, head cocked. "Don't we have enough unopened boxes in the house? You had to bring in another?"

I narrowed my eyes. "Are you busting my chops for not unpacking faster?"

"I would never."

"You so would," I muttered. "Sometimes I think you can actually channel Gil's thoughts." I looked down at Gil. He was sitting upright with his fluffy tail curled around his front paws, observing Avi and me out of slitted eyes. "Although the only reason he wants me to empty boxes is so he can sit in them."

"Then we shouldn't keep him waiting. What have you got?"

"As I was saying," I drawled, flicking my gaze between Avi and Gil, "when Ricky and I came out of the falafel place, I noticed there was an occult supply shop next door. I thought it might be a good connection for Patrice, so we stopped in and Ricky gave the proprietor one of the psychic knitting shop manager's cards."

"You realize it's not a psychic knitting shop, right? There's no such thing as psychic knitting."

I lifted a brow. "Many people would say there's no such thing as ghosts."

"Hmmm." Avi rubbed the back of his neck. "Fair point."

"Don't worry." I gestured from myself to Gil. "Nobody in *this* house is so ill-informed."

"Much appreciated," he said, his expression matching Gil's.

"*Anyway*, the visit to that shop was incidental. The important thing was the flyer posted on the board outside the shop." I patted the box. "For a company that sells paranormal investigation equipment."

Avi frowned. "A little disrespectful, isn't it? To post something so adversarial right by a store that sells supplies to encourage preternatural relationships?"

"I thought that, too. But it gave me an idea. I mean, whatever paranormal investigators do once they've identified a potential hot spot, they have to have some way to find it in the first place, right? To verify that something supernatural exists?"

"Yes. So that they can *exterminate* it. That's why they're called ghost *hunters*."

I shook my head. "Not necessarily. Some of these folks are just looking for a connection. Communication. Proof of life." I waggled one hand. "Well, proof of afterlife, I suppose. But to do that, they need a way to facilitate that proof more objectively than Victorian spiritualists like Thaddeus Richdale used sketchy mediums. In other words, technology." I patted the box. "So I checked out their website and ordered a few gadgets."

"Do I need to point out that you don't require any of those gadgets, Maz? You're communicating just fine."

"Yes." I met his gaze. "But you aren't."

He blinked. "What?"

"You can't speak to anybody but me." Gil mewed. "Well, me and Gil. What if we could find a way for you to speak to other people? To Saul? Patrice? Taryn? You wouldn't have to be so dependent on me."

I couldn't identify the expression Avi's face. Was it hurt? Anxiety? Hell, was it betrayal? "Am I imposing on you? Asking too much? I could—"

"No! No, that's not it. This isn't for my benefit at all. It's for yours." I slid the box toward me and placed my palms on its sides. "You can't interact with most physical objects other than paper and sawdust. That might change over time, but right now, you're limited by that. You can use the Smith Corona, but not easily."

"That's putting it mildly."

"One of the gadgets I ordered is a voice-to-text recorder based on radio frequencies. If we could identify your frequency, if you could record your voice, you could dictate a new book and I could transcribe it for you. Avi." I leaned over the box, the pressure of my hands making it flex. "You could *write* again."

Okay, *that* expression I could read—a desperate hope and longing that he pushed aside immediately.

"Why should I bother? You won't even take the royalties for the old books. There hardly seems any point to writing more of them."

"The point is that writing is your calling. You keep saying we don't know how this works and you're right. But you could be around for a long time, Avi. Maybe longer than I will."

He flinched. "I… never thought of that."

"Can you really face eternity with nothing at all to do? Won't that get tedious?" I paused, struck by a thought. "Come to think of it, maybe that's why ghosts act out over time. Pure, unadulterated boredom." I forced myself away from that tangent and met his gaze squarely, because this was *important*.

"Please, Avi. It's been ten years. Don't you have new stories to tell? Don't you want other people to read them?"

Avi's shoulders rose and fell. "I... I'd like that. I think. But maybe not as Jake Fields. A new pen name. A new genre. Then you could publish them as yourself and—"

"Nope. I'll be your assistant, but I won't take credit for your work. Publication details can wait, but I'm sure Taryn can help with that. It'll give her another chance to conspire with your agent. What this"—I tapped the box with two fingers—"will do, what I *hope* it will do, is enable your *process* again. To give you a reason to be *present,* even if I'm not around. But it's totally your call. If you don't want to—"

"No! I'd like to try. But I also need to get used to the idea, you know?"

"Sure. I get it. In the meantime, if you need a reason to hang out when I'm not here?" I pointed to Gil. "Keeping Gil company is clearly a priority. At least to him."

Avi chuckled. "Far be it from me to disappoint Gil."

"Exactly. Now let's see what's in this box, shall we?" I opened the drawer I had mentally labeled *miscellaneous sharp thingies* and brandished the box knife. "Behold. The right tool for the job."

I slit the tape on the top of the box and folded the flaps aside, giving silent thanks that the company used bubble wrap rather than foam peanuts as packing material. When I lifted out the top sheet, Gil practically teleported to the countertop.

I grinned at Avi. "Check this out."

I let the bubble wrap drift to the floor, and Gil jumped onto it immediately, batting the bubbles with his claws partly extended. When he managed to pop one, his tail lashed, and he leaped backward before zooming across the kitchen floor, barely skittering to a stop next to the dishwasher. Then he lowered his belly to the ground and crept forward until he was a foot from the bubble wrap, his rear end wiggling before he pounced.

As I unpacked the box, Avi watched Gil go through the same routine again and again.

"Does he do this often?"

I shrugged as I lifted the voice-to-text recorder out of the box and set it carefully on the counter. "What can I say? Some cats go bonkers for catnip. Gil has a thing for bubble wrap." I glanced down at him as he popped another bubble and zipped across the room. "Although he never says no to catnip either."

After unpacking the EVP portal and setting the faraday bags aside, I stored the rest of the bubble wrap with the reusable shopping bags and set the box on the floor. Gil froze in the act of murdering another plastic bubble and leaped inside to peer out at us from the gap between the top flaps.

"That's him set for the next hour or so." I nudged the red and black boxes toward Avi. "This is the recorder and a device that's supposed to extend its reach and scan for radio frequencies. If we can identify your, um, hertz, then we can use this to increase the draw."

Avi leaned forward, resting his elbows two inches above the countertop. "How does it work?"

"Good question. Let's find out."

Unlike my dad, who'd considered any new gadget a direct challenge to figure out—he'd always started by smelling the object, for some reason—I always read instruction manuals, even though the spelling and syntax errors in many of them made me cringe. Dad enjoyed the journey of discovery, no matter how long it took or how many detours he followed, but if I'd gone to the trouble of buying something, I wanted to be able to use it properly as soon as possible.

I opened the recorder's box and a flimsy paperback booklet thicker than *The Manual of Style* dropped out. "Uh... This might be more complicated than I thought."

Avi laughed. "Does the other one have an instructional tome as well?"

I peeked inside the portal box. "Yep."

"You have to go back to work soon, right?"

"I don't *have* to, but I probably should. I ran across a promising lead this morning, and I'd like to follow up."

"Then how about this? Since paper is on my short list of manipulable items, leave the manuals here. I'll read them and brief you on them tonight." He frowned. "No. Not tonight. You have a date with Ricky, don't you?"

I smacked my forehead. "Crap. You're right."

He dropped his chin and gave me a severe look from over his glasses. "That's not the attitude you should have when you're granted the opportunity to spend time with your boo."

"My boo?" I snorted. "Was that ghost humor?"

"Unintentional, I assure you. However…" Glancing aside, he gnawed on his lower lip. "I'd like to try something while you're gone."

"Okay. What do you need from me?"

"That's it? You don't even want to know what it is?"

I shrugged. "I doubt it's going to involve human sacrifice or anything, so of course I'll help."

"Maz." Somehow, he managed to lace my name with both fondness and reprimand. "Do you ever *not* jump into things without looking first?"

"What?"

"Never mind." He straightened. "We know I can't join you at the Manor, so there's no point taking Oren's ring with you. What if you left it in Sofia's house?"

"I don't know." It was my turn to chew on my lip, frowning as I gazed out the window toward Sofia's lawn. "Didn't you think it, well, *activated* because I'm a little bit Oren? It might not work without my presence."

"Maybe, but we're not sure, and that's the point. This is the perfect time to test it, though. Nobody's at Sofia's place. It's nearby. If you leave the ring inside and I'm able to move between here and there, that will tell us something. Then we can start testing other variables, too."

"That's... actually a really good idea."

"Let's try it now before you have to go back to the Manor. And if it does work, you should take the manuals and Gil over there, too."

I frowned. "The manuals I get, but why Gil?"

"Seriously, Maz? You have to ask?" He gave me a pitying look. "You and Ricky deserve some privacy or you'll *never* get to first base, let alone second or third."

"Great." I rolled my eyes. "I'm getting hookup advice from a ghost."

He spread his hands. "If the shoe fits..."

"Fine. We'll bring Gil." I pointed at him. "But this isn't because I'm looking for a booty call."

"Mmm-hmmm."

"I mean it, Avi. This is just so we can see if I'm a necessary part of the equation. I'm not even sure it will work."

"It will work." He folded his arms. "Trust me. I've got a feeling."

"It's never going to work," I muttered, as I retrieved Gil's visiting-Sofia go-bag.

"Stop complaining, Maz." He followed me out of the kitchen door, Gil's carrier in my hand. "It will work."

"It won't."

"It will."

"It won't."

"It will."

"It won't."

What can I say? It worked.

CHAPTER TWENTY

As much as I wanted to dive into a comparison of Frances's journal and the housekeeper's ledgers the minute I got back to the Manor, I ran headfirst into two logistical problems. First, I didn't actually *have* the journal, and wouldn't until we either got the physical copy back from the bookbinder or they forwarded us high-res images of the pages. However, I remembered the dates the journal covered perfectly well, bringing me to the second logistical problem.

The ledgers didn't appear to cover any of the same dates.

I couldn't just go tearing through the rest of the crates in search of more journals or additional ledgers. Well, I mean I *could*, but the point of my job was to *organize* the papers. If I abandoned my methods of discovery and categorization now— I'd managed to get through maybe a tenth of Thaddeus's crates so far—I'd jeopardize my progress, which would be a disservice to Saul and the Manor.

Also, while the crates themselves hadn't been in any particular order, their contents *usually* had some relationship to each other, either because of category or relative date. So instead of rampaging through the room like a berserk tornado, I did the responsible thing and logged the contents of the box I'd opened that morning.

I was rewarded for my adulting win when the last pages of the final ledger in the stack coincided with the first three days covered by Frances's journal. Maybe, if I was very persuasive— or sicced Saul on them—I could get the bookbinder to send me the images of those pages now rather than when the final project was delivered.

In any case, I took pictures of the ledger pages with my phone so I could start brainstorming some blog posts.

The housekeeper, whose name was never written, started every day's entry with a list of who was resident in the Manor at that time. Considering how tight a rein Frances apparently held over the household finances, this might have been a way for the housekeeper to justify the expenses for housing, feeding, and entertaining the family of eight along with a throng that could vary from zero to more than twenty.

A lot of people traipsed in and out of the Manor in those days. I tapped my dusty fingers on the desk. What about a series of profiles? Character sketches not only of the Richdales—that was a no-brainer—but of their guests as well? They could have been notable Ghost residents back then. At the very least, they were people that the Richdale family felt were important enough to invite to their home—I flipped through a few ledger pages—often for weeks at a time. Why? Why them? And why specifically at those times?

Like many men of his era, Thaddeus was all about money and the power that marched along with it. Presumably he'd sought both in the ordinary way of hammering out profitable partnerships and crushing his competitors underfoot before he became laser-focused on wresting the location of Josiah's alleged treasure from beyond the veil and immersed himself in spiritualism.

Given Frances's acerbic introduction to her journal, her goals were vastly different, probably around social position and influence. She had two sons and four daughters, more than enough fodder for founding a dynasty through advantageous marriages.

Wait. Why *wasn't* there a Richdale dynasty?

Why hadn't any Richdale heir come forward to lay a claim to the Manor or Thaddeus's other assets—I glanced sidelong at the mountain of crates—such as they were?

What had happened to the Richdale children? To Jasper and Daisy and Iris and Violet and Cornelius and Caroline? Why were there no Richdale grandchildren? No nieces or nephews? No cousins?

Cousins. *Crap.*

I checked the time on my phone. I needed to get home, shower, and change so I could pick up Ricky for our so-not-a-booty-call date. I made a quick note so I wouldn't forget this line of investigation, locked up, and headed home.

As I was driving down Main Street, my gaze caught on the Taqueria, the pub, the psychic knitting shop, the library.

Right. The library.

I smacked the steering wheel with both palms. If I wanted to know what happened to the Richdales, I could just *ask*. Saul, as director of the Manor, probably knew everything, and if he didn't—well, his husband was the town's volunteer librarian. Whatever Saul didn't know, Jerry would.

That didn't really change my plans for posts about the family and their guests, but it might make research much easier, not to mention less dusty. Once Saul and Jerry got back from their mini-vacation, I'd talk to them both and see whether they felt like the profile pieces would be of interest. I mean, they'd be of interest to *me*, but I didn't want to just yodel into the void. I wanted the posts to have a wide enough appeal that they'd benefit the Manor, benefit the town.

I sighed, and since I'd be driving Ricky's truck to Richdale, I pulled the Civic into the garage and made sure the door had cycled closed before I stepped into the mudroom. I expected Gil's usual demanding greeting since it was close to his dinner time, but there was nothing.

Oh, right. He was next door with Avi.

Neither Gil nor Avi took up a lot of physical space, but the house felt so *empty* without them here that I crept up the stairs, almost afraid to make any noise.

When I got to the top of the stairs, I rolled my eyes. "What is wrong with me? It's not like the house has *another* ghost. Get hold of yourself, Amani."

I marched into the bathroom and turned on the shower. Even if this was totally not a booty call date, I owed it to Ricky to look less like a dust Yeti. By the time I got downstairs, clean again and in a fresh pair of jeans and long-sleeved T-shirt in a color Greg had always referred to as "Rose? Are you kidding me?", my curls were still wet, but at least they weren't frosted with document detritus.

The EVP equipment, still in its original packaging, sat on the counter. After a moment's consideration, I moved them to the butler's pantry. If Avi decided he didn't want to experiment with the devices? I wouldn't push. As much as I wanted more stories from him, whether in his Jake Fields persona or a new one, the next steps were in his hands. He had little enough agency nowadays. I wanted to let him take the lead whenever he could.

I glanced at the clock on the wall over the sink. Felicia had texted me that the best time to ambush Ricky would be around seven, at the nurse's shift change. Their charge nurse cousin would be back on shift then and would support me in getting Ricky out from underfoot.

Her words, not mine.

I hadn't ever been to the hospital in Richdale. In fact, I hadn't been to Richdale at all other than to drive through it on the way to and from Portland. It'd take me an hour at most, and it was only five thirty, so I had half an hour to kill.

I was tempted to head next door to see how Avi and Gil were doing at Sofia's place, but I resisted, because *agency*. I could unpack one of the boxes Ricky and I had hauled back from Greg's place, but I'd been buried in Thaddeus Richdale's past all day and surrounded by Oren's past for weeks. I wasn't ready to face my own quite yet, even if the scope was considerably less intimidating.

Then again, when it came to facing your past, it was quality, not quantity, that was more likely to kick you in the gut, right?

However, maybe I could handle a *little* bit of the past—just a taste—if only to keep me company without even Gil around. I decided to throw together one of the comfort foods from my childhood—my dad's chickpea salad, a recipe that I knew from memory. Ricky and I could share it tonight, since I suspected he could use all the comfort he could get.

Two cans of chickpeas were draining in the sink, and I'd finished chopping the parsley and green pepper when Avi appeared across the island from me. I squeaked and dropped the onion.

"Crap!"

"Sorry," he said. "I thought you'd be used to me by now."

"No worries." I caught the onion before it rolled off the countertop. "I was kind of lost in thought." I gestured to the vegetables, the jar of olive oil, the lemons waiting to be squeezed. "This was one of my dad's signature dishes. It's bringing back memories."

"Ah. Memories." He tucked his thumbs in his cardigan's pockets. "I can understand that. I've encountered my share this afternoon, too."

I halved the onion and started to dice it, trying to keep my fingers curled under for safety the way Dad had taught me—and mostly failing, just as I always had. The onion's fumes were muted since I'd chucked it in the freezer for a few minutes first, so I couldn't blame them for the tear that trickled down my nose. I wiped it away with the back of my wrist. "Did you spend much time at Sofia's back when... when..."

He lifted a brow. "When I was alive?"

"Well. Yeah."

"I did. She's lived in that house as long as I can remember, although I never knew her first husband. When I was a kid, she was still taking an active role at the restaurant, so she wasn't around during the days so much. My parents and I often spent evenings there with her and Ramon."

"Ricky's uncle?"

"Yes. Lorenzo, Liam's father, was already an adult by that time, though. I attended his wedding, in fact."

"Really?"

He nodded. "Remember, I'm more than ten years older than Liam. I was there the first time Lorenzo and Susanne brought the baby to visit Sofia. She was ecstatic, even though he screamed the whole time."

"Well, neither of those things has changed," I murmured. Sofia still doted unconditionally and Liam still expected the stars to align for his own convenience. When it came to family, some lessons could never be unlearned.

While others never stuck, no matter how hard you tried.

I paused with my hand on a lemon, my fingers tightening as I stared at the unevenly chopped peppers and onions, the mangled parsley. *Other lessons never stuck, no matter how hard you tried.*

"I don't know what I'm doing."

Avi peered at me, his forehead knotted in concern. "What?"

"My dad could cut vegetables so precisely they were like clockwork gears. Ricky's family makes food like music." I pushed the lemon away. "He'll hate this."

I picked up the bench knife, but before I could start scraping my pathetic vegetables into the compost bucket, Avi was there in front of me. I could have barged through him, but I wouldn't. I couldn't, any more than I'd knock over anybody else who stood in my path.

"Stop it, Maz."

"Why? It's nothing but a salad, Avi."

"So? He'll like it. I promise."

I tossed the bench knife onto the counter with a clatter. "It's not even *hot*."

"He'll like it because you made it."

"I don't want him to eat it out of *pity* or... or *obligation*."

"If I know one thing about the Vargas clan, it's that for them, eating the food isn't the point. The taste, the presentation. Those have value, sure, but they're secondary. *Sharing the meal* is what's important." Avi's gaze was intense, but so kind I had to swallow twice. "He'll *love* it because you made it *for him*."

I turned away from him and braced my hands on the countertop. "Then I guess I need to get over myself, huh?"

"No." Avi moved to the other side of the counter and sat by folding himself onto the barstool. "You told me once that everybody is entitled to process grief in their own way, and that you never know when it can hit you again. I think that over the past few days, it's hit you again."

I rubbed the center of my chest, the same way I'd seen Avi do. "You think?"

"I do. You confronted Greg, and no matter how toxic that relationship was when it ended, you still invested your emotional capital in it."

I scoffed. "You can't know that." Greg had certainly claimed otherwise.

"I know because I know you. You throw yourself into things for people you care about." Avi gestured to himself. "Even people you haven't known for long." He traced his wedding band with a finger. "Even people you never knew at all."

I swiped a hand under my eyes. "I'm being ridiculous."

"You're not. And I'm sorry."

The obvious sorrow in his tone made me look up. "For what?"

"That Oren never found you."

I gripped the edge of the counter, focusing on the tumble of vegetables next to my hands. "Do you think he ever actually looked?"

"I don't know. The last time I saw Oren's will, your mother was the only named beneficiary. But he was—" Avi looked away, his throat working. "He was the most caring man I ever knew. He wouldn't have intentionally abandoned you." He gestured to the salad ingredients. "Any more than your father did. Any more than Sofia would." A corner of his mouth twitched. "Not even a certain family member who's completely undeserving of her devotion."

I sighed, my shoulders sagging. "Well, I'll give Liam a bit of credit. At least he showed up. I expect that'll mean more to Sofia than anything else."

"It will help. Sofia may borderline worship Liam, but love isn't a zero-sum game for her. She gives the Vargases just as much, every one of them."

"Yeah, but just *look* at them." I flung my arms out. "They *deserve* it."

"So do you! And it is not your fault that Oren didn't contact you."

"It might be. It probably is," I grumbled. "It usually is."

"Honestly. Stop gaslighting yourself. Stop letting *Greg* gaslight you when he's not even in the picture anymore. He's not entitled to any of your headspace ever again." He pointed to the counter. "Now dress the fricking salad and go collect the man who *does* deserve the headspace." He waggled his eyebrows. "As well as space in other places, including your bed."

I clapped my hands over my ears. "Stop! What do I have to do to convince you this is not a booty call?"

"Maybe finish the salad?" He stood. "I'm going back next door."

I blinked. "Oh. Hey. I forgot to ask how that was going."

"I'll forgive you this once." He gestured to himself. "Since I'm standing here, you can deduce that I can at least return home. But I've popped back and forth several times." He chuckled. "That seems to confuse Gil a bit, but he's always waiting for me wherever I pop back in. It's like he has a special sense and can predict where I'll appear."

"Wait." My eyebrows dipped. "You're not just appearing next to the ring?"

"No. It's a different spot in the house every time."

I drummed the counter. "Hmmm."

Avi's eyes narrowed. "There's that lightbulb look again."

Lightbulb, hunh? In this case, he was right on the money. "Did you consider that it might be the other way around?"

"What do you mean?"

"As brilliant as Gil is, he's not psychic. I don't think he's predicting you." I waggled my fingers at him. "I think *you're* homing in on *him*. The same way you can home in on the ring." I pointed to the floor. "Or this house. They're like... anchors, I guess? Tethers? Something you can use to pull yourself out of wherever you are when you're not manifesting."

His eyebrows rose and he blinked. "You might have something there." He made a shooing motion with both hands. "You. Go. Pick up Ricky. I'll try a few more things. See if I can consciously pick what anchor I choose or what tether I pull. Regardless, neither Gil nor I will be interrupting you tonight, so be sure you take advantage of that fact."

"It's not a booty—" But he was gone. I exhaled sharply as I eyed the vegetables. "Evidently, I could use a little comfort tonight, booty or not. So I might as well finish the freaking salad."

CHAPTER TWENTY-ONE

"You know," Ricky said as he dumped more salad into his bowl, "this is really good."

The disclaimer—*it's not as good as my dad's*—was hovering right on the tip of my tongue, but at the last moment, I remembered Avi's words and just said, "Thanks. I'm glad you like it."

"Are you kidding?" He grinned. "I love it."

And you know something? I didn't care whether he loved it because it tasted good or just because I'd made it for him. I'd shared something that mattered to *me* and it mattered to him, too.

That was enough to kindle a warmth in my chest that crept up my neck and burned in my cheeks.

As though something had just occurred to him, Ricky paused, his fork hovering in front of his mouth, and looked around the room. "Hey, where's Gil? I'm not used to eating here without him watching my every bite."

It struck me that Ricky might not appreciate Avi and me using Sofia's house for our experiments with her in the hospital. "He's, ah, contained elsewhere. With Avi. We're alone."

I buried a wince. Did that sound creepy? That sounded creepy. I released a shaky breath when Ricky didn't stare at me like I was the second coming of Norman Bates.

Think. Think. What to talk about?

"So. Um. I've been wondering about something." He didn't stop eating, but his eyebrows rose as though inviting my question. "Liam is our age, right? About thirty?"

"Thirty-one. His birthday is on the cusp and his mother kept him back from starting kindergarten for a year so he'd be bigger for sports." Ricky snorted. "Not that it mattered. He hated sports."

"Sports aversion aside, thirty-one is a little beyond the standard age for getting a bachelor's."

"He took a gap year. Or six. Didn't go back to school until his mother remarried and moved to Athens with her new husband."

"Athens, Georgia? Liam didn't go with them?"

Ricky gave me a glance over the rim of his water glass. "Athens, Greece. And no, the new stepfather wasn't a fan. He let Liam take his last name but drew the line at funding his lifestyle."

"Ah. Well, in any case, Sofia must have been glad to see him today." I chased my last chickpea around my bowl.

Since Ricky was busy chewing, he mumbled, "Mmmphmm?"

I smirked. "Don't choke. I'll wait."

Ricky managed to laugh and swallow at the same time. "Liam's in town?" I nodded as he scraped up the last mouthful of salad. "Mami must have called him after all, even though Tia didn't want to *bother him*." Although he didn't make the standard hand gestures—one hand was still occupied with his fork—I could hear the air quotes in his words.

"Yeah. He showed up here, and Felicia directed him to the hospital. Didn't you see him?"

He shook his head. "He must have stopped in while I was doing a dinner run for Mami and Papi." He wiped his mouth with his napkin. "Glad I missed him. He'd have probably tried to talk Tia out of the procedure, just like he always does, which wouldn't have been great for my blood pressure."

I decided not to mention Liam's reaction, nor his threats to me. If Ricky hadn't had to face them himself, I could at least spare him that. "Did her doctors give her an ultimatum this time? Is that why she decided to go through with it? You told me surgery makes her nervous."

"It does. That's why Mami and Papi are sitting with her tonight. Tio Lorenzo died after surgery following his heart attack." He scowled at his empty bowl. "Liam never misses a chance to remind her that she was the one who convinced Susanne to let the doctors operate. He contends that Tio would have recovered on his own."

"Would he?"

Ricky snorted. "Not a chance. Massive coronary. He coded twice on the way to the hospital. But Liam has Tia half believing that surgery equals death."

"So why did she agree to do it this time?"

"For the same reason she hasn't before—Liam. Since the recovery time is short, she'll be able to travel to Boston as planned for Liam's graduation. She declared she wasn't going to miss that." He cupped his hands around the base of his glass, shaking his head with a rueful expression. "If it stabilizes her condition, it may be the only thing I'd ever thank that pendejo for."

"I—"

I broke off when Ricky's jaw nearly cracked with a massive yawn. He ducked his head, pink infusing his cheeks.

"Sorry. It's not the company. I promise."

I chuckled. "Don't worry. I don't take it personally. However..." I caught his gaze. "I'm under orders to make sure you sleep."

Ricky scrubbed his hands over his face. "That's easier said than done. Every time I close my eyes, I see Tia lying there in the garden."

"Would it..." I swallowed, a phrase from my mom's favorite classic *Doonesbury* strip playing in my head: *And the kid goes for broke*. "Would it be easier if you slept with somebody else?"

Ricky froze and then peeked out from between his fingers. "You mean... with you?"

I nodded. "If you want to. If it would help." I held up my hands, palms out. "No other shenanigans on the table. Or in the bed. Not unless you, um, wanted that." The regret that etched unfamiliar lines in his face gave me my answer before he opened his mouth, so I plunged ahead. "I get it if you're not that into me, or whatever, but I'm really just talking about comfort and companionship right now. About not being alone."

He dropped his chin and stared at his open palms for a moment. "Maz. You know how you have an ex?"

"Yeah. Unfortunately." Several, in fact.

"Well, I have an ex, too."

I choked on air. "What? When? How did—" Shaking my head, I said, "Never mind. You don't owe me any explanations."

"I know I don't owe you any. Nobody *owes* anybody things they'd rather keep private. But I'd like you to understand." He reached out. I took the invitation, placing my hand in his. "I like you. So much. I have from the first time we met. But that's how it started with Blaine, too. I rushed into things. *We* rushed into things, didn't take the time to learn enough about each other to know how to build a solid relationship. And without that foundation?" He shrugged. "It fell apart in a really painful way."

I winced. "Trust me, I get it. I'm sorry you had to go through that."

"I'm not telling you this for sympathy." His lips trembled, but a smile didn't quite make it through. "Although I won't turn it down. I'm telling you so you'll understand why I want to build our foundation first. Because if we don't take that time, the end... Well, I don't want to think about how awful it could be."

I could see his point. With my house, with Avi, I was fixed here in Ghost for good. Ricky's roots here went even deeper, his family so interwoven with the community that I didn't think they *could* be separated.

"I understand. And no pressure. I, um, really like you too." I gestured to the room around us. "I'm clearly not going anywhere. So I'm happy to take all the time you need—"

"That *we* need."

"That *we* need to build our foundation. But, Ricky?"

"Yeah?"

"If you ever want to talk about your ex, about what happened, I'm here. Okay?"

"Okay." He took a shaky breath. "In that case—"

A knock sounded at the door and I held up one finger. "Hold that thought. I'll be right back."

I hurried out of the kitchen. When I got to the family room and had a clear shot to the front door, I slowed down a little. The person I spotted through the fanlight was vaguely familiar, but then I placed her. So, despite her visit derailing the conversation with Ricky, I was smiling when I opened the door to Ghost's resident sheriff's deputy.

"Hey, Kamilla. How are you doing?"

Her answering smile was tight. "I'm fine, Maz, but this isn't a social call."

My belly clenched and my hand tightened on the doorknob. "What's wrong?" Had Liam already launched his campaign against me? I didn't think a civil suit, even one that was justified —which his wasn't—warranted arrest.

"Is Ricky here?"

"I—"

"Kamilla?" Ricky appeared at my shoulder. "What is it? Did something happen with Tia?"

"You could say so." Her handcuffs jingled as she pulled them out of her belt pouch. "Enrique Vargas, I'm arresting you on the charge of attempted murder."

CHAPTER TWENTY-TWO

To say I was gobsmacked was an understatement. "Attempted murder? What in the *what*? Of whom?" Because even gobsmacked, grammar had me by the throat.

"Of Sofia Vargas."

I expected Ricky to protest. Strongly. Using adult language. In his outside voice. But instead, his eyes widened and his skin went positively gray.

"Ricky?" I whispered.

"What happened? Kamilla? What did I miss?" He stumbled forward, his fingers curling into fists. "What did I *do*?"

"Who says you did anything?" I turned to Kamilla. "You know this is wrong. He'd never hurt Sofia."

Kamilla pressed her lips into a flat line. "What I feel isn't relevant, Maz. This is my job. Do you think you could let me do it? If Ricky comes along *quietly*"—she glared meaningly at Ricky, and I realized she hadn't Mirandized him yet—"it will help more in the long run."

Ricky peered up at me from under his lashes. "It's all right, Maz." He held out his arms, his hands relaxed.

"Do… Do you have to cuff him?"

Kamilla didn't answer, but as she snapped the handcuffs on Ricky's wrists, she gave me an apologetic look. "I'm taking him to the sheriff's office in Richdale for booking. In case you need to let anybody know."

I stood on the porch, the door open behind me, watching as Kamilla took Ricky's arm and led him to the waiting patrol car.

"This can't be happening." Then Kamilla's words hit me: "*In case you need to let anybody know.*"

Of *course* Ricky wouldn't contact anybody, let alone a lawyer. For one thing, he was exhausted and not thinking clearly. For another, he'd flat out said it was *his fault.*

"For cripes' sake, Ricky," I muttered as I pulled out my phone and dialed Taryn, "keep your mouth shut."

After three rings, Taryn answered. "Maz. This had better be good. Haley and I are in the middle of—"

"Ricky was just arrested," I blurted.

"What? Why?"

"For attempting to murder Sofia."

"Oh, for the love of... Where are you?"

"I'm at my house, but Kamilla said she was taking him to the sheriff's office in Richdale for booking." I paced to the end of the porch and looked across the lawn at Sofia's house. "Taryn, you *know* he would never do anything to hurt Sofia."

"Of course I know that."

"But he feels responsible for her, for everything that happens to her. I'm just afraid that if he doesn't have somebody with him, he'll say something hideously suspicious just because he feels like he should have somehow prevented her collapse. I mean, it's not like any of his family or I can be with him while he's questioned. Your dad is still out of town and he doesn't practice anymore, anyway. You're the only other lawyer I know. Will you do it, Taryn? Can you go be with him? Help him?"

She sighed audibly. "I'm not a criminal defense attorney, Maz."

"But you *are* an attorney. I'm just a freaking ghostwriter. There's... there's nothing I can do for him." I swallowed thickly and tried to laugh. Unsuccessfully. "Hell, the way Liam was tossing threats around, I'm surprised they didn't arrest *me.*"

"Wait. Liam's in town?"

"Yeah. Ricky said his mom must have called him, even though Sofia didn't want to *bother* him."

Taryn snorted. "Not likely. Maria *always* caves to Sofia about everything except how many peppers to add to the salsa."

"Well, somebody did."

There was a brief pause, where I heard another voice murmuring to her. *Crap*. Haley. I'd barged in on them again. "I'm sorry. I'll—"

"Don't be. You did the right thing. I can head to the sheriff's office now. With luck, he won't have said anything incriminating yet."

"Too late for that. He practically told Kamilla he was at fault."

"Damn it, Ricky," she muttered. "Fine. With luck, I can keep him from digging a deeper hole. I can at least be there to advise him, and even if I can't represent him at trial, I know people who can. Don't worry."

"Can you... That is, attorney-client privilege and all that, but can you call me and tell me *why* they think he's their suspect? And why they think it's a murder charge?"

"If he gives me permission, I can let you know about our conversation. I'll call you as soon as I know something."

"I appreciate it. I'm sorry I interrupted your date."

"Are you kidding? If you hadn't interrupted us, neither of us would have ever forgiven you." Another soft murmur. "Well, okay, we'd have forgiven you. But groveling would have been necessary, and only if Ricky said it was okay."

I sagged against the porch railing. "Thanks, Taryn."

"There's no need to thank me, although I should definitely thank you. For looking out for Ricky. I'm glad he's got somebody like you in his corner."

"Just make sure he doesn't paint himself into one and we'll call it even, okay?"

"You got it. I've got to go."

I let my hand drop to my side, still clutching the phone like a lifeline. I needed Gil in my arms to steady me, but he was still with Avi. I trudged to the other end of the porch and dropped onto the swing. It swayed under me as I propped my elbows on my knees and let my head fall forward.

I don't know how long I sat there, but it must have been at least an hour, because when Taryn called me back, she was already in Richdale.

Before I could choke out a question, she said, "I haven't seen him yet. He's still in booking. But I know what the charges are and why they suspect Ricky."

"That's so ridiculous. Ricky would never—"

"Maz. They were debating whether to arrest you, too."

"Me? Wh— Oh, did Liam accuse me after all?"

"No. He had nothing to do with it. Sofia collapsed because somebody tampered with her medication."

"Did the pharmacy make a mistake?"

"No. The new bottle was fine and had all the expected pills in it. The previous bottle was missing, so they assume it had already been discarded. But the remaining pills in the case cause an increase in heart rate, the opposite of what she should be taking for her condition." She took an audible breath. "The only fingerprints on the new bottle and the pill minder were Ricky's." She took another breath. "And yours."

"But... but..." How did they even *have* my fingerpr— Oh, right. My TSA known-traveler number. It had been so long since I'd flown anywhere that I'd forgotten about it.

"The EMTs said you're the one who brought the medications to the ambulance, so they're only considering you a possible person of interest right now. Depending, I suppose, on whether Ricky blurts out another nonspecific confession."

"Don't let him do that, okay?"

"I'll do my best. Talk soon."

I set the phone on the seat next to me and buried my face in my hands. There was no way that Ricky would have replaced Sofia's meds any more than I would have. But if Taryn wasn't able to keep him from incriminating himself, or worse, taking a plea deal for something he didn't do, he could be convicted for it, anyway.

For that matter, would he be tempted to confess to protect *me*? Based on the forensics, I was the only other potential suspect at the moment.

"Maz? Is this a bad time?"

The soft male voice was vaguely familiar, so I pushed away the urge to snarl. When I looked up, Dominik and Jillie Vlahos were standing on my walk, at the foot of the porch steps. I pushed my curls off my forehead and forced the facsimile of a smile.

"No worries. What can I do for you?"

"Bernadette sent us to check out a few things in your kitchen so she'll know what to expect when she cooks for us here tomorrow."

I winced. *Crap*. I'd invited the Vlahoses for dinner, and I'd forgotten about it completely.

"If you need to reschedule…" Dominik said slowly.

"No. No, it's fine." Maybe forcing myself to be marginally sociable would keep me from mental doomscrolling 24/7. "If Bernadette wants to scope out the kitchen, I'm surprised she didn't come herself."

"She wants to be *surprised*." Jillie's voice was loaded with weariness more suited to a middle school teacher the week before spring break. "You know. By the whole house at once. If she just sees the kitchen today, she thinks it will… It will…" She looked up at her uncle. "What did she call it?"

He smiled down at her. "Lessen the wow factor."

"Yeah. That." She met my gaze. "Mom gets kinda weird sometimes."

"Don't we all," I murmured. I stood up. "Come on in."

As the Vlahoses mounted the steps, Jillie pointed to the swing. "Uncle Dom, can we get a porch swing for Jenkins House?"

"We already have a gazebo. It has bench seats all the way around it."

"Yes, but that's in the backyard. This could be on the front porch." She gazed up at him with wide puppy-dog eyes. "Please?"

"I've got to say," I said, "it's one of my favorite parts about this place." I chuckled a little weakly. "Of course, all parts of the place are my favorites. That happens when you get a windfall like this." I opened the door wide since I didn't have to worry about Gil making a run for it, and gestured for them to enter. "Be my guest."

As Jillie passed me, she was humming "Be Our Guest," and Dominik, following on her heels, spread his palms. "She's been singing that ever since we signed the papers. I think she's more excited about running a B & B than Bernadette and me, and we've been fantasizing about it for years."

I stepped inside to find that Jillie had frozen in the middle of the entry, staring through the french doors opposite the stairway. "You have a *library*."

Her enthusiasm was so infectious that it pulled a real grin out of me. "I do."

She turned to Dominik. "Uncle Dom, can we—"

"Hold your horses, Jillie-bean."

She scowled at him. "Don't call me that. That's a kid's name."

"Then stop acting like a kid." Dominik scrunched up his face. "No. You know what? Go ahead. Act like a kid as much as you want."

She pointed through the doors. "Do you mind?"

"Not a bit."

She walked through the doors and squealed. "It has *window seats*! Uncle Dom, can we—"

"Put it on your list, Jillie." He shot me a sidelong glance and mouthed *her very long list*. "We'll talk about it later." After she sprinted across the room and flung herself onto the window seat, Dominik gestured for me to step back out of sight. His expression was a combination of defensive and embarrassed. "Sorry. She's just really excited to finally nest. While I was away at college, she and Bernadette moved three times in five years, trying to keep one step ahead of Bernadette's ex. Every time she thought she'd shaken him, he'd show up again, like some drug-resistant bacteria."

"He's stalking her?"

"He's extorting her. Trying to squeeze money out of her by threatening to sue for custody of Jillie." He snorted. "As if. No family court judge with half an ethic would let that guy near a kid, and now that I'm back, he'll keep his distance again." He leaned closer and dropped his voice. "Jillie doesn't know. I probably shouldn't have said anything, but I didn't want you to judge her too harshly or think she's some entitled brat."

Although terror for Ricky had all but paralyzed me, I managed a smile. "No worries there. She seems like a great kid."

His shoulders dropped about an inch as tension visibly drained from him. "Thanks. She is. But we shouldn't take up more of your time. Jillie," he called, "let's keep moving. We still have to stop at the bakery."

"Okay." Jillie made the word sound as though she was the furthest possible from okay.

"Drama llama," Dominik said. "Comes with being eleven."

Sure enough, when Jillie emerged from the library, she was dragging her feet as though they weighed a ton. Each. But then she spotted one of Gil's catnip mice and bloomed like a morning glory.

"You have a *cat*?"

"I do. His name's Gilgamesh. Gil."

She turned to her uncle. "Uncle Dom, can we get—"

"Jillie. Slow your roll. We'll talk about it after we've had more than ten minutes to settle in, okay?"

She faced me again, her clasped her hands under her chin. "Can I meet Gil? Please?"

"You can tomorrow. He's not here right now. Visiting next door."

"With Mrs. Vargas? Is she better now? We had dinner at the Taqueria last night and they said she was in the hospital." She scrunched her face just as Dominik had. "I hope she doesn't have to deal with that blond *jerk* right after she's been sick."

"Jillie!" Dominik said. "Manners."

"What? It's not like you thought he was nice, either."

My eyebrows shot up. "Blond jerk? What— Oh, right. You were here when Liam arrived, weren't you?"

Jillie bobbed her head emphatically, her nose still wrinkled. "Yeah, but I saw him before that. Like a week before. While Mom and Uncle Dom were talking to the B & B owners."

I glanced between Dominik and Jillie. "But... Aren't you the B & B owners?"

She gave the typical pre-teen *seriously-can-you-believe-how-clueless-adults-are* eye-roll. "Not *ours*. The one in *Richdale*."

"There's a B & B in Richdale?"

Dominik nodded. "The people who run it are really nice. They offered to let us pick their brains about the business." He nudged Jillie's shoulder with his elbow. "But we didn't make Jillie listen to all the boring logistical talk."

She gave another epic eye-roll. "I *told* you, Uncle Dom. I don't mind. I *want* to know this stuff. Jenkins House is gonna be my home, too." She grinned, a little slyly. "But the muffins were really good that morning, so I decided to pass on the meeting and just grill you both later. Plus, it gave me a chance to observe the breakfast service. And *that*"—she punctuated the word with a jab of her finger toward me—"is where I saw the blond je— that guy. He rolled into the room and started complaining about everything. The coffee. The muffins. The bacon."

Dominik frowned. "They didn't serve bacon."

"I *know*," Jillie said. "*That's* what he was complaining about. He insisted that they make some for him." She peered up at the ceiling as though she expected a replay of the scene to unroll there. "I'm not sure, but I *think* they had to send someone out to buy some, because the server disappeared for a while before I smelled bacon cooking. That je— guy spent the entire time sitting at the only six-top in the room *by himself* and scrolling through his phone. He even took a call once and talked really loud about legal stuff."

My jaw had slowly dropped as Jillie spoke. I snapped it with a click of teeth. "Let me get this right. Liam was in Richdale a week ago? Are you sure?"

Jillie nodded. "Positive. Plus, the server told me he'd already been there for two days and was making everyone's life hell—"

"Jillie," Dominik said with the time-honored parental-equivalent warning tone.

"What? It's what they said, and it's not like we believe in that superstitious stuff, anyway. I think that's why the owners were so glad to meet with you and Mom all the time. It gave them a chance to get away from him."

I pinched the bridge of my nose, doing the mental math as heat built in my chest and behind my eyes. Nine days. Liam had been in Richdale for nine days.

Never mind what he was doing in Oregon during the last weeks of his final semester—class requirements could vary, after all. But Sofia maintained an entire *suite* for him and set a place at her table for him at every meal, yet he'd chosen to stay an hour away at a B & B, for Pete's sake.

He'd been there when he'd chastised her for losing her phone. When he'd thrown shade at her for inconveniencing him during graduation week just by being in the same city. Hell, when she'd collapsed in the garden and been *hospitalized*.

Liam was Sofia's only blood relative, and she'd financed his entire Harvard education *in cash*, yet he didn't bother to show up even once to share a meal or give her a hug or just say hello. If he'd been terrorizing the poor B & B hosts in Richdale for *nine freaking days*, he should have had plenty of opportunities to pop over to Ghost for an hour or two. Granted, it might have cut into his busy bacon-eating/phone-scrolling time, but was it too much to ask for him to make the effort?

Ice rolled through me from throat to belly.

What if he had *made the effort*? What if he'd made the effort *more than once*?

Taryn told me that Ricky's and my fingerprints were the only ones on the bottles and pill minder. But with two of the case's compartments open, there was another set of prints that should have been there but were notably absent.

Sofia's.

CHAPTER TWENTY-THREE

When Ricky had passed Sofia her prescription refill on the day we'd planted her garden, it had still been in the white pharmacy bag. To get the bottle into the medicine chest, Sofia would have had to touch it. She'd have had to touch the pill minder to open the empty compartments.

So why weren't her fingerprints present on the bottle and the case?

Obvious answer: Somebody had wiped them down.

Now let's see... Who might be invested in doing such a thing? How about another obvious answer: Liam, who'd been less than subtle about suggesting that Sofia wasn't competent to take care of herself. What better way to prove his point than to make it look as though she couldn't manage her medications at the same time as he'd been making a nuisance of himself in Richdale, conveniently within Porsche key-fob distance when Sofia had collapsed in her garden.

Had he intended for Ricky to be accused? Maybe. Maybe not. I didn't like the guy, but I could give him the benefit of *that* doubt, as well as the one that whispered he'd intended to actually kill Sofia. I think this was just another way for him to gaslight her.

But why here? Why now? Had Sofia's impending trip to Cambridge been the catalyst? If so, Ricky had been right. The guy was a total asshole. Also, it meant that this wasn't Ricky's fault, whatever he thought.

It was mine.

Kamilla should *have arrested me, after all.*

E.J. RUSSELL

No, screw that. If Liam had done this, it was his fault, and he needed to answer for it. Now.

"I'm sorry. I need to make a phone call. The kitchen's down that way, through the family room. Go ahead and take a look. I'll join you shortly."

I waited for them to disappear into the kitchen, accompanied by oohs and aahs from Jillie, then called Felicia.

"Hey, Maz. What's up? I hope you convinced Ricky to eat."

Gah! Obviously she didn't know about the arrest, and no way was I breaking that bit of news. "As a matter of fact, I did. I wanted to ask you a question, though."

"Shoot."

"Do you know who called Liam to tell him about Sofia?"

"Ricky."

"You sure?"

"Uh huh. When I told Mami and Papi that I'd seen him at your house, they weren't happy, since Tia told them not to tell him. They thought Antonio might have done it from the hospital, but Mami is Tia's emergency contact, so he didn't. Besides, Antonio thinks Guillermo is a tool." She chortled. "His words, not mine. He said he was glad he didn't have to deal with him in the ward."

"And nobody else is likely to have done it?"

"No. Besides, Guill—*Liam* said Ricky called him when we saw him on the lawn. Remember?"

"Ah. That's right. Thanks."

"No problem. Anything else?"

"No. That's it."

"Okay. Bye!"

Yep. Totally my fault. The only reason Liam was in town was because Sofia told him about the trip. She'd told us he kept trying to talk her out of it. In fact, we'd heard it ourselves on the first call.

Was he really that ashamed of his family that he'd go to these lengths to hide them from his Harvard friends? I remembered

Liam's rant on my front lawn, and Jillie's tales of his behavior in Richdale.

Who was I kidding? "It's all about him, the entitled, narcissistic asshole. Of *course* he'd go to these lengths."

Dominik poked his head out of the kitchen. "Did you say something, Maz?"

"Sorry. Just talking to myself." I tried to arrange my face into a less disgusted expression. "Will the kitchen meet Bernadette's needs?"

He grinned. "A six-burner gas range and an acre of end-grain cutting board? You may never pry her out of it."

Jillie joined him in the doorway. "Uncle Dom, Jenkins House has almost the same thing, except it has *two* six-burner ranges."

"I suppose that makes sense," I said. "Oren did design both kitchens."

Jillie held up a flat copper pan that ordinarily hung in the butler's pantry. "Is it okay if I take this to Mom? She was planning to make paella, and if she can prep it in the pan before we come over, she can just pop the whole thing in the oven and we can eat sooner." She hugged the pan to her middle. "Trust me. You totally want to eat sooner. Mom's paella is *awesome*."

"By all means, take it with you." I shifted from foot to foot, the urgency of needing to contact Kamilla and tell her my suspicions probably making me look like I needed to duck into one of the house's many bathrooms, *stat*.

Dominik clearly picked up on it. "Come on, Jillie. We've imposed on Maz long enough."

"Oh, that's not so." My voice sounded weak, even to me, and Dominik laughed.

"You don't have to pretend. We'll see you tomorrow at six." His expression turned serious. "But if you need to cancel for any reason, just call." He pulled a business card from the pocket of his olive green button down and handed it to me. "That's the Jenkins House front desk. One of us will answer it."

"Or at least collect the message," Jillie piped up, "because Mom is always puttering in the kitchen and Uncle Dom is usually swearing at the computer about bank balances."

"And that's enough out of you, madam." Dominik placed his hand at the small of Jillie's back and propelled her down the hall. "We'll see ourselves out."

He opened the door and stepped onto the porch, but Jillie broke away from him and turned back toward me, clearly about to have the last word. Before she could say anything, though, Avi appeared by my side.

"Maz!" His hair looked like he'd been through a whirlwind, and the cover of a paperback I'd left on the sofa started to flutter. "You have to come quickly. Something's happening."

A *clang* echoed from the porch, and Dominik's admonishing, "Careful, Jillie!" was cut off by the snick of the closing door.

"What is it? Avi? What's wrong?"

But Avi wasn't looking at me anymore. Instead, he was staring at the door, a look of utter shock on his face.

"Avi?" I flexed my fingers, irked that I wasn't able to touch him to draw his attention back to me. I decided to try for decibel shock. "Avi!"

He flinched. "You don't have to shout."

"Apparently I do, because you weren't answering. What's going on?"

He shook himself, like a dog emerging from a lake. "So much. I'll tell you. But Maz?" His voice held a note that I'd never heard from him before.

"Yeah?"

"I can't be certain, but I'm pretty sure..." He met my gaze, his eyes wide. "I'm pretty sure that kid could see me."

CHAPTER TWENTY-FOUR

"Seriously? That's great!" I started for the door. "I'll call them back and we can—"

"Maz. Stop. That doesn't matter now."

I turned back to see Avi wringing his hands. "One more person who can see you? Of course it matters. Plus, it doubles our data points. If we can figure out what differentiates us from people who *can't* see you, then—"

"Yeah, sure. Fine. Whatever." Impatience and irritation warred with something like flat-out terror on his face. "But that's for later. What matters now is what's happening next door."

"Next door? In Sofia's house?"

"Yes, Maz. In Sofia's house. Where I've been all day."

I frowned. "There's no need to get snarky. Er."

"There is, if it means you'll *listen*."

I held up my palms and patted the air. "You're right. I'm sorry. What's going on?"

"Liam is in the house."

"Liam? But we locked everything up. How did he get in?"

Avi gave me a flat stare. "How do you think?"

I slapped my forehead. "A key. Of course he has a key." I'd seen his damn keychain—the gold charm had nearly embedded itself in my nose. "He's got his own suite upstairs. Maybe he's finally relocated from the B & B in Richdale." I stalked into the kitchen and peered out the turret windows at Sofia's house. "Although it would have been better if he'd showed up when she was actually *there*," I muttered.

Avi, right on my heels, obviously heard me. "If that were the case, wouldn't he be *in* his suite instead of Sofia's room? Wouldn't he be bringing luggage *in* instead of taking things *out*?"

I gawked at him. "He's taking things *out*?"

"That's what I just *said*." Avi stamped a transparent foot, making no sound. "Maz, Oren's ring is there, lying right on the window ledge over the sink. What if he sees it? What if he takes it? He's taking her other jewelry. Just grabbing it by the handful, not even looking at it. If he takes Oren's ring—"

My knees wobbled and I planted my palm on the table to steady myself. "You won't be able to leave the house again."

"No! If he takes Oren's ring, it will be *gone*."

"Okay. Okay." I strode out of the kitchen, through the family room, and into the library, drumming my fingers against my leg. When I knelt on the window seat and scanned the road, I couldn't spot the silver Porsche anywhere. "We've got to do something. But what?" I scrambled off the window seat, startling Avi, who'd been standing right behind me. "Can you get back over there?"

He nodded. "As long as he hasn't already taken the ring away."

"Has he taken anything out of the house yet? Anything at all?"

"No. He's just shoving things into a suitcase he found in Sofia's room."

A suitcase. Her new suitcase. The one Felicia had convinced her to buy for the trip to Cambridge. I curled my fingers into my palms. "You know, I've never hit anybody in my life, but I really, *really* want to punch this guy."

"You wouldn't be the first," Avi growled. "Oren *hated* him."

"If we didn't already know Oren had great taste, that would have sealed it. Can you..." Avi had a very peculiar look on his face. "What?"

"Nothing. It's not important now."

"No. Avi, tell me."

He looked away and I could swear his transparent face took on a pink tinge, like the promise of sunrise. "You've complimented me on my writing. But that's the first time you've complimented *me*."

"I... What?" I rewound my remarks. *Oh*. "I stand by that. Oren had fantastic taste, especially in his choice of partner. Now, can you check on Liam again? Since he probably has every right to be in the house for legit purposes, we need to get proof that he's there for sketchy reasons."

"The stolen jewelry isn't enough?"

"Not until he actually takes it. I didn't see Carson's car on the street anywhere, but—"

"Why would Carson's car be on the street?"

I lifted my eyebrows. "Because Liam is driving it. You saw it the other day, parked in front of the house."

Avi shook his head. "That wasn't Carson's car. It had Washington plates."

I frowned. "Are you sure?"

"Positive. I can check again, if you like. He parked in Sofia's garage, and I can get there. I tested my maximum radius earlier today, and it's well within access range."

"Can you check the plate number for me? Memorize it and let me know?"

He nodded. "I should. Wait here." He vanished.

"Crap." I kept forgetting about Avi's ghostly teleportation powers. I raced into the kitchen and dug in the junk drawer for a pencil. I found one, but no paper, so I retrieved a torn envelope from the recycling bin. Just in time, too, because Avi popped back in, repeating the plate number over and over.

I hurriedly jotted it down. "Got it. Can you go keep an eye on him? Let me know if he's getting ready to leave or if he's doing other shady stuff." I picked up the envelope. "I'm about to overstep in a big way."

"Why? What are you going to do?"

"I'm about to activate the Vargas cousin network." I held up my right hand. "For good, not evil, I promise."

Avi's smile was a little tremulous. "I'd never doubt it." He disappeared again.

I blew out a breath, and with the plate number in hand, called the Richdale sheriff's office. "Hello? Could I speak to Yaz, please?"

"This is Yaz." Yaz's voice was an indeterminate timbre—high tenor? Low alto? Not that it mattered.

"Yaz, my name is Maz Amani."

"Oh." Their voice warmed. "Ricky's friend."

"Yes." I had to clear my throat because if the cousin network knew about me, that meant that Ricky—or someone else in the massive clan—had talked about me. "I'm about to ask for something that might be a little, well, illegal?"

"You realize you're speaking to the sheriff's office, right?" Their careful tone didn't contain a hint of sarcasm.

"I know. And I'm not sure if this is in your purview or not, and if it isn't, please say no, but I promise this is something that will help Ricky."

"Anything I discover outside the investigation won't be admissible. It could compromise the case."

"If so, just tell me, and I'll drop it. But I'm going to give you a Washington license plate number. Could you run it and tell me who the car is registered to and what the address is?"

"Is the car parked illegally?"

"Nnnooo."

"Is it engaged in illegal activity?"

"Potentially, yes."

"What's the number?"

I read it off and Yaz said, "You think this will help Ricky?"

"Pretty sure. Yes."

"One moment, please."

I don't think I breathed for the entire time Yaz had me on hold. Then they were back on the line, and what they told me was a game changer.

Well, except for my desire to punch Liam. If anything, that had escalated.

Ex-po-nentially.

CHAPTER TWENTY-FIVE

"Seattle?" I roared when Avi reappeared next to me in the kitchen. "That douchecanoe lives in *Seattle*. His car's been registered there for three years." No wonder he'd been able to show up in Richdale within a few hours of getting Sofia's call about the Harvard graduation trip. "Hell, does he even *go* to Harvard?"

Avi dodged out of my way as my enraged pacing took me around the island. "Maybe you could find out. There must be a student directory."

"Yes, but because of privacy issues, you can't access it unless you're a student or an alumnus. I found that out during a ghostwriting gig a couple of years ago, and unfortunately, I don't know any of those."

Avi set his jaw. "Yes, you do."

"You? You went to UO. We hung your diploma on the attic wall."

"Not me. Professor DeHaven."

I blinked. "Patrice went to Harvard?"

He nodded. "Double major in comparative religion and folklore and mythology."

A double major from Harvard? This made Patrice even more intimidating, but my fears didn't matter. Not now.

"I'll call her and see if she'll check. Was Liam still there?"

Avi hesitated for an instant, then nodded. "He just put that new cell phone Ricky bought her the other day in the suitcase."

I growled, low in my throat. "What do you bet he took her others, too? Snuck in and swiped them just to make her think she'd lost them?"

"No bet," he said flatly.

"Keep an eye on him again? I told Yaz that something might be going down here, so they're going to alert Kamilla, but we have to have something concrete for her before she makes a move. Give me maybe five, ten minutes and then come back and report?"

He nodded and popped out.

I wasn't familiar with Patrice's teaching schedule, so I just dialed her number and hoped she'd be available.

She answered on the first ring. "Maz? Is there another manifestation?"

"Yes and no. We've got something to tell you about, but that's not why I called. I have a huge favor to ask."

Patrice's chuckle was decidedly rusty. "You're the sole conduit to the first spiritus manifestation in Ghost. There's little I wouldn't do for you. How can I help?"

"I understand you went to Harvard, and that as an alumna, you have access to the online student directory."

"That's correct."

"Could you check on a current student for me? He should be graduating this month."

"Name?"

I grimaced. Crap. What name would he be using? I had no idea what Sofia's first husband's last name had been, but I'd bet Gil's kibble Liam wouldn't be using it, nor *Guillermo* either. What was his stepfather's name again? Ricky had told me, but — *Got it.* "Frost. Liam Frost. Possibly William Frost."

"One moment please."

While I was waiting, Avi returned, looking nearly as angry as I felt. *"What?"* I mouthed. He just shook his head and wrapped his arms around his middle.

"I'm sorry, Maz, but there is no student by that name, graduating or otherwise."

"Thank you," I said woodenly.

"You're welcome. I look forward to hearing about the latest developments whenever you're ready." She disconnected the call.

Not one for social niceties, Patrice. It was one of the things I most admired about her.

I set my phone on the counter gently, because if I threw it against the wall and shattered it, I'd release some frustration now, but trade it for the aggravation of replacing the phone later.

On the other hand, maybe I'd be able to score one from Liam. He evidently had a few extra lying around.

"So." I planted my palms against the counter. "We know why Liam was so against Sofia coming to his graduation. He's not graduating."

"He's failed out of Harvard? But isn't he supposed to start law school?"

"He didn't fail out. He's not even a student. I doubt he's ever set foot in Cambridge or anywhere else in Massachusetts, his stupid gold keychain notwithstanding. That jerkwad has been scamming Sofia out of more than a hundred grand a year for *four freaking years*." No wonder he could afford a Porsche, not to mention a place in Capitol Hill.

"He's about to keep doing it, too."

"What do you mean?"

"He has one of those big light boxes, the kind you can use to trace drawings? He's using it to trace Sofia's signature onto a check. For a hundred grand."

"Son of a—" I slapped the counter. "How the hell does he think he can get away with something like that? I mean, he doesn't even need to. If he asked, she'd probably just hand him the money, no questions asked. He's *everything* to her." I didn't want to think about what it would do to Sofia to find out Liam had been lying to her for years. "She was so *proud* of him."

"That might be why. You know what Carson was like. Liam is cut from the same cloth. Their image of themselves is more important than anything else."

I froze. "Carson. Crap. *Carson*. One second." I scrabbled my phone back into my hand and called Taryn.

"Maz—"

"Yeah, yeah. Whatever I'm interrupting, I'm sorry, but this is critical and *really* time sensitive. You know how Sofia shelled out for Harvard tuition for Liam?"

"Yeeeaaahh," she drawled, aggravation giving the word about six extra syllables.

"Short story—he's not now and never has been a student. He's been living in Seattle this whole time on her money."

"Are you kidding me?"

"Not even a little. Plus, tuition checks were made out to Liam, not the school, and Sofia never mailed them." I scrunched up my face and slapped my forehead. "Of *course* he wouldn't let her mail them. He didn't have a Cambridge address."

"Still in the dark here," Taryn said.

"Right. Sorry. The way Liam got those checks? Sofia gave them to Carson--who *allegedly* was attending annual conferences in Boston—to pass along."

There was a moment of silence, and then—as I knew she would—Taryn got it. "Carson was complicit in the fraud."

"*Exactly*. I don't know how possible it is for someone to speak to Carson like in the next hour, but I suspect he'd turn on his ol' buddy in a heartbeat if it means he can cut a deal on his own charges."

Taryn literally growled. "I can't promise anything, but I'll make some calls."

"Could you make one of those to Kamilla? She's already on her way, but she may need more to make the arrest."

"On it."

After she hung up I took a deep breath, letting the tension—a very little bit of the tension—drain out of me. But then I got a good look at the grim lines bracketing Avi's mouth.

"What?"

"I think I know how Liam was planning to get away with it. How he still might, if Taryn can't get to Carson in time."

I gritted my teeth. "This is bound to be good."

"The big light box was a tight fit in his messenger bag, and when he finally wrestled it out, some… other things spilled out too. A pill bottle."

"Prescription?"

Avi nodded. "The patient name on the label was smudged, but the expiration date was over a decade old. I recognized the drug because my father had a heart condition. It increases the heart rate."

A couple of memories pinged my brain. "Liam's father. He died because of heart disease."

"He did. He had the same issues as my dad and ignored them just as resolutely."

"Dammit!" Slapping the counter wasn't enough, but punching it wouldn't do anything but break my knuckles. "Not only did he monkey with Sofia's meds, he did it with expired drugs. Who *knows* what that could have done? Were you able to"—I made a shooing motion with both hands—"nudge the bottle under a chair or something so there's evidence with *his* freaking fingerprints?"

He shook his head. "You know I can't affect physical objects. Much. But a lot of papers spilled out too." He waggled his fingers. "Papers I can handle, so I looked while he was setting up his little forgery workshop. On… on her kitchen table." Avi's voice broke, and my own throat seized up.

The kitchen table. Where Sofia set a place for Liam—for *Guillermo*—at every freaking meal.

"Go on," I managed to choke out.

"A conservatorship petition, citing a danger to herself or others. An advanced directive plus medical power of attorney. In other words, he'd have sole authority over Sofia's assets and medical care."

"No way. *Gil* is more a danger to others than she is. And Maria has her medical POA. Sofia would never sign anything like that."

He pressed his lips into a thin line. "She doesn't have to sign them, does she?"

My stomach dive-bombed my toes. "The light box. He's going to forge her signatures on those, too."

He nodded. "I tried to stall him. I was able to"—he waved his hand through the air—"disrupt the electrical circuit in the light box a couple of times, but it wasn't fatal. He got it to cycle back on."

"Dammit," I muttered.

"But, Maz. There's something else."

"Something worse than him trying to victimize his own grandmother?"

"Well, maybe not that, but you be the judge." Avi's Adam's apple bobbed. "He came in through the back door. It didn't latch."

My head swam as if I'd stood up too quickly. "Gil?" I croaked.

Avi nodded. "The light box was padded with bubble wrap and Liam tossed it on the floor. Gil—"

I pressed the heels of my hands against my eyes. "Gil pounced."

"Yes. And popped a bubble. Liam jumped nearly a foot before he figured out it was Gil and not, I don't know, a gunshot. When he shouted and lunged for him, Gil darted outside. Liam slammed the door then. I manifested on the porch, but he must have run outside my range so I couldn't find him. I'm sorry, Maz."

I took a deep, shaky breath. "It's… Well, it's not okay, but we'll deal with that later. He hates sharp movements, especially from strangers, so it makes sense that he'd hide."

Avi nodded, still looking absolutely miserable. "When I got back inside, Liam was lining the power of attorney up on the light box and talking on the phone. I could only hear half of the conversation, but I think he was talking to an appraiser."

I ground my teeth together. "For Sofia's jewelry?"

"No. For Sofia's house."

My jaw sagged. "Her *house*?"

Avi nodded. "He said he wanted everything settled so the house could go on the market ASAP."

"That rat *bastard*."

"We can't let him get away."

"You're damn right." I grabbed my phone again. "Let me know if he tries to bolt?"

Not bothering to reply, Avi vanished.

I pulled up my recent calls and dialed Yaz. "It's a go. Tell Kamilla to hurry."

"Copy that. But it could be at least fifteen minutes. She's still on her way back to Ghost."

"Thanks, Yaz. We'll be on the lookout for her."

Avi returned. "He's on the move. Shoving everything back in the messenger bag."

"Crap." I chewed on my lower lip. "We've got to stall him somehow." My gaze zeroed in on the garage door, across the mudroom from where we stood. I bared my teeth at Avi. "Feel like a road trip?"

He returned my feral grin. "I call shotgun."

CHAPTER TWENTY-SIX

I glanced over at Avi in the passenger seat as the garage door rolled up behind the Civic's rear bumper. I almost told him to fasten his seat belt as mine clicked into place. "Ready?"

"Wait." Avi swiveled to face me, one of his knees passing through the gearshift. "What is your plan, exactly? You shouldn't confront him inside the house. That could give him a way to shift blame onto you."

"How could he do that? *I'm* not the one who's forging Sofia's signature and trying to declare her non compos mentis."

"No, but he could muddy the waters, and we want these waters totally clear, don't we?"

"Very true. But I wasn't planning to face him at all." Because there was no way I could resist punching him, and then he *could* cast blame on me. "Sofia's garage is a single-wide, so if I park in the driveway, I can block him in."

"That'll infuriate him."

"Good," I growled as I turned the key in the ignition. It caught the first time. "That'll make two of us."

"Don't you mean… three?"

I met Avi's evil grin, threw the car into reverse, and hit the gas.

The Civic skidded on the driveway gravel as its rear wheels cleared the garage. Yes, my tire treads were pathetic, but I probably shouldn't punch the gas this hard or I'd be making an unscheduled appearance in Patrice's sitting room.

I eased up on the pedal as I finished backing out. I shifted into Drive. "Hold on."

There was no answer, and when I glanced to my right, Avi was gone. *Crap*. We weren't in his domain anymore and we must be outside of the ring's radius. But I couldn't stop to check on him. Liam had been packing up. If he'd already left the house, we couldn't afford another delay.

Could Liam run faster than I could drive? He didn't have as far to go, but I wasn't an Indy 500 driver by any stretch, and my car wasn't exactly a Formula 1. So I headed down the driveway and pulled onto Iris Lane, hoping that Avi wasn't stuck *elsewhere* and that he'd be able to rejoin me once I was back in range.

Gunning the engine, I peeled off down the road, taking the turn on to Birch Street way too fast. The Civic groaned, tires squealing, as I yanked the wheel straight. Sofia's garage door was up, but I couldn't see Liam's car. Was I too late? Had he already left?

I punched it again and huffed a relieved breath when I spotted the silver trunk. Hunching over the wheel, I braked hard as I turned into Sofia's driveway and screeched to a halt smack in the middle. Liam wouldn't be able to maneuver his way out on either side of me, even if he was willing to scrape his paint all to hell. He'd need some way to collapse his Porsche into a concertina if he wanted to escape, and since he wasn't Mr. Incredible, I doubted he'd be able to pull that off.

As I switched off my ignition, Avi blinked into sight in the passenger seat again.

"You okay?"

He nodded. "Just a little disoriented."

I gestured to the garage. "Was the door up when you checked out the license plate?"

"No. I... don't think so? I wasn't really focusing on that when I was trying to remember the numbers."

I scanned Birch Street. No sign of Kamilla yet. "His car's windows are too dark for me to see the interior. Did he already make it to the garage?"

"I don't know. Once you backed out of the garage, I was *elsewhere* before I showed up back in our attic. I know he's not in Sofia's house anymore because I popped in there first." Avi *tsk*ed. "He left the back door hanging open. You'd think he was born in a barn."

"So the ring's still on the windowsill?"

"Yes." The relief in Avi's voice was palpable. "I didn't follow him outside, though. I'll check now."

"You don't have to—" But he was already gone.

The Porsche's brake lights flared. "Uh oh."

Through my open window, I heard a muffled click. And another. And another, followed by some very creative cursing, but no sound of the engine.

Avi. He's interrupting the ignition.

Pride swelled in my chest. He was making such great progress, not only in mapping his current abilities, but in embracing new ones. Is this what parents felt like when their kids mastered a skill?

"Watch out, EVP devices, because Avi Felder is in the hou—"

The Porsche's engine roared, and Avi flashed into the passenger seat.

"Maz! Jump!"

"*Crap!*"

I wrenched the handle and *shoved*. As usual, the damn door stuck.

"Come on, come on." I threw my weight behind my shoulder and bashed it again. It didn't budge at first and I heard the Porsche's engine rev once, twice, three times. "Come *on*, dammit!"

Something flew past my face and suddenly I was tumbling out of the car and rolling across the ground, gravel digging into my arms, back, and finally chest as I came to a halt, face down, just as the Porsche crashed into the Civic with a deafening *wham* and a sickening *crunch*.

Avi appeared, kneeling next to me, his chest heaving. He peered down worriedly. "Are you okay?"

"I'm fine. Is he getting away?"

"Not in his car, he's not."

"He could still run." I tried to push myself up. *Nope. Not happening.* "We have to stop him."

Avi glanced away for a moment before gazing down at me. His smug smile was hampered by his ragged breathing. "I think that's taken care of."

"What? But—" Flashing blue light washed through Avi and into my eyes as Kamilla's patrol car screeched to a halt at the curb, blocking the end of the driveway. She and another officer were out of the vehicle in an instant.

"Maz? You all right?" she called.

I lifted one hand in a feeble wave. "Never better. Don't mind me."

"Is he armed?"

"No gun." Avi wheezed. "Or knife."

"If you're wrong—"

"I'm not."

"Not armed," I replied to Kamilla. "But he's got a lot of stolen property on him, so watch out for him trying to destroy it."

"Got it." She disappeared into the garage, and a moment later, I heard her recite the familiar Miranda words in a clipped tone, followed by Liam's curses.

Avi peered down into my face. "Are you sure you're fine?"

"Fine-ish." I gritted my teeth, pushed myself onto my hands and knees, and then sat back on my heels. "Damn. I'm gonna feel that tomorrow." I flashed him a pained grin. "Ziv Harcourt may have no trouble jumping out of moving cars, but even a stationary one is tough for me."

"Harcourt is a fictional character." Avi was still trying to catch his breath, which interfered with his usual acerbic tone. "You're not."

I squinted at him in the twilight. "Are *you* okay? You're panting like you just ran the 400 meters at an Olympic pace."

"I... I don't know." He stared past my shoulder. "I think I just opened your car door."

"What?" I twisted to look behind me and *ow!* Yeah, that was a mistake.

"When I saw that you were stuck, and that Liam was going to ram you, I just"—he thrust his hands forward—"and it opened. You might have done it yourself and it was just a coincidence, but—"

"Nope. I was well and truly stuck." I peered at my palms and dislodged a couple of pieces of gravel, a grin slowly dawning. "Avi, my friend, you are no longer restricted to manipulating only dust, cat fur, and paper products. You've just added metal to your repertoire."

He gazed at me, lips parted and eyes luminous, even though periodically washed by blue light. "What if it was just a one-time thing?" he murmured. "A response to an imminent threat of death or serious injury, not something I can consciously control?"

I met his gaze. "As *someone* recently said to me, stop gaslighting yourself. You've got this." I pointed to his wedding band. "Metal, remember? You're just getting started."

CHAPTER TWENTY-SEVEN

Somehow, despite being pitted in unfortunate places by gravel, I managed to push myself up until I could wobble onto my feet. I was upright in time to see the glorious sight of Kamilla frog-marching Liam out of the garage and turning him to the wall. This time, when she produced her cuffs, I didn't protest—they couldn't get slapped onto a nicer guy.

As the cuffs clicked home, Liam's clenched fists uncurled, and his keys dropped to the ground. Still on slightly dizzy autopilot, I bent down to retrieve them to hand to her partner.

"Please leave those where they are, Maz." She gave me a tight-lipped smile as she gripped Liam's arm and turned him toward her cruiser. "Chain of evidence. You understand."

Since her partner was approaching with a giant roll of yellow crime scene tape, I said, "Right. Got it."

"The house will be off limits for a while too, until we clear it."

As she walked past, I murmured to Avi, "Is there much left in the house for them to see?"

"No. Everything's in the messenger bag and the suitcase."

That was both good and bad. Good, because Kamilla would have the evidence of Liam's assholery prepackaged in a couple of nice, neat containers. Bad, because he could just as easily say that Sofia had given him permission to take everything, and somehow, even if she were confronted with proof of his lies and theft, I doubted she would ever deny him.

Luckily—or unluckily, if you were Liam—unlike civil crimes, in Oregon, criminal charges like grand larceny weren't something the victim could ask to be dropped.

"Please step away," the partner said.

"Sorry."

I backed up so he could unroll more tape, enclosing where Liam's keys had fallen. Its charm flared and faded, flared and faded, in the still-flashing blue light. I squinted down at it, because now that it wasn't an inch from my nose, I could see it better.

"That's not Massachusetts," I blurted.

Liam shot me a look that would have burned out my eyes if he'd been an actual demon rather than simply having the withered soul of one. "Shut your damn mouth."

Kamilla stopped and lifted an eyebrow. "Now, why would that matter to you, Liam? Maz? Do you have something else that might be germane to the case?"

"When Liam practically impaled my nose with his keys—"

"I never touched you!"

"No. You didn't. But you gave me a closeup view of your keychain. At the time, I thought whoever made it didn't do a very good job of rendering Massachusetts, but it's not Massachusetts." Nor, despite what that geography app's lousy photo tagging claimed, was it a microwave oven. "That's Belize."

Liam just glared at me and turned away, his neck flushing an alarming shade of red.

"Is that significant in some way?" Kamilla asked.

"Ricky told me that Sofia was the victim of identity theft a few years ago, and the thing that raised the red flag was the thousands of dollars charged to her credit card from a resort in Belize." I gave Liam a glare of my own because, jeez, was he a piece of shit. "I'd suggest that when you're preparing the case against him, you investigate that incident. Saul should be able to help you. He's the one who resolved the issue."

She nodded sharply. "Thanks. We'll check it out."

Avi appeared in front of me, so I watched Kamilla escort Liam to the curb filtered by his body. "Tell her about the pill bottle."

"Kamilla?"

She didn't answer until she'd settled Liam into the cruiser's back seat and shut the door. "Yes?"

"I'm pretty sure you'll find pills that match Sofia's incorrect meds in his bag."

"Should I ask how you know that?"

I spread my hands, palms up. "This is Ghost."

She narrowed her eyes. "Hmmm. I suppose the evidence will speak for itself, but we'll need your testimony."

"You've got it. Ricky's cleared, though, right?"

She nodded. "In light of the new information, he should be, once the investigation is concluded. In the meantime, he's being released. If you want, you can pick him up in Richdale in about two hours."

The relief that swept me made my knees threaten to fold. "I'll be there."

She climbed into the car, but leaned out before closing the door. "And Maz? Thanks."

"No problem."

Beside me, Avi snorted. Since I was still trying not to butt-plant in front of the deputies, I waited until the cruiser pulled away from the curb and turned onto Iris Lane.

I turned to him. "What was that snort for?"

"Your *no problem* comment. Clearly, your definition of *problem* needs work, Mr. Ghostwriter, because this whole day has been nothing but one of them stacked on top of another."

He had a point. "I was just being polite."

"In cases of police investigation, you might want to aim for precision over politeness, but at the moment, you've got another… shall we say, difficulty to add to the mix."

My belly jolted. I wasn't sure I could handle anything else right now, because although Liam had been apprehended before he could do Sofia even more harm, and Ricky was about to be freed, Gil was still missing.

"What other difficulty?"

"You told Kamilla you'd pick Ricky up."

"Yeah?"

He inclined his head at the yellow tape that fluttered in the slight breeze. "That could be a challenge."

I grimaced. "Right. My car's a part of the crime scene. Awkward."

"That's not exactly what I meant." Avi flicked his fingers over my shoulder. "Given your rather disorienting exit from the car and the subsequent excitement, I'm not certain you've taken in the full magnitude of the scene."

"Hunh?"

"Look behind you, Maz. The only way you're getting to Richdale is if you hitch a ride on a tow truck."

I turned slowly and sucked in a sharp breath through clenched teeth. I knew that sudden traumatic events could interfere with short-term memory, but how in *blazes* had I missed this? Denial, maybe?

Because the front of my poor Civic was completely crumpled, Liam's Porsche embedded in its bumper and grill. I wasn't a mechanical expert, but even I could recognize a total when I saw one. Although I'd managed to remain upright while the police were here, I sank to the ground and dropped my head into my hands.

"Well, crap," I muttered. "I guess I'm getting a new car after all."

CHAPTER TWENTY-EIGHT

I handed Ricky a glass of iced tea as he stood at the window in my breakfast nook, looking out through the blinds at where Sofia sat on her porch.

He accepted the glass. "Gracias."

It had been three days since Liam's arrest, two since Sofia's ablation. Maria hadn't told her about it before the procedure. She'd left it to Ricky to break the news afterward, which had kind of pissed me off until Ricky had told me it had been his choice.

We were all in a holding pattern now, even Avi and I. I'd postponed the dinner with the Vlahoses, because Avi was having trouble assimilating the changes to his existence over the last few days.

"Even if I could, I'm not ready to talk to somebody new yet," he'd said. Then, with a wry smile, he'd added, "I'm not sure I want to talk to you right now either. I need a little... space. Time to get a handle on all of this. If that's all right with you."

"Sure, Avi. Take all the time you need."

He'd offered to just stay in the attic while they were there, but that didn't seem right to me, so I'd canceled, and the Vlahoses were very gracious about it.

"We're not going anywhere," Dominik had said. "There's no rush."

Ricky was still shaken too, not just by his own experience, but by Sofia's close calls at Liam's hands. Although he put a good face on it, claiming to be fine, I knew he was more affected than he appeared because he hadn't once mentioned taking me to visit his cousin the car dealer.

To be honest, I was feeling a little fragile at the moment too, because Gil still hadn't shown up. I spent almost as much time walking the streets of Ghost calling his name as Sofia spent in her rocking chair, gazing out at her garden.

I gestured toward her with my tea, the glass cold against my palm. "How's she doing?"

"Not great. She says it's not necessary for me to stay with her now that she's recovered from the surgery, but when I promised not to hover, she didn't object. I think she was relieved not to be alone."

"You can hardly blame her. She's got to be heartbroken after finding out that Liam's been lying to her and stealing from her for all these years. She's lavished all that love on a completely undeserving asshole."

He shrugged. "She hasn't stopped, you know. She says he needs that love now more than ever. She doesn't hold it against the rest of us that we aren't as forgiving, though."

I watched Sofia rocking, rocking, rocking, and a drop of condensation trickled over my fingers. "You know, I vetted a book for this social worker once. She was the director of a mental health clinic, so she had to deal with staffing issues across all the programs they offered. She told me about this mid-level manager who she wasn't sure was up to the job, but she said, *'I just pretended he could do it.'*"

"What good would that do? If he was incompetent, shouldn't she just get rid of him?"

I smiled down at him, wanting to smooth the crease between his brows, but after his confession about his ex, I resisted. "It wasn't as critical as that. He was capable, just... rough-edged. With that mindset, though, she interacted with him from a place of perceived success, not expected failure."

"Did it work?"

"She said so. Client care stayed at a high level, which was her goal. But I think the effect on her own well-being—coming from a positive rather than a negative place—was the bigger win."

"That's Tia. She always believes the best of everyone." He sighed. "She wanted to pay his lawyer fees, did you know?" When I shook my head, he continued. "But Taryn's friend is handling it pro bono."

"Sure he is," I muttered.

He turned his head sharply, his eyes wide with shock. "What do you mean?"

Oops. Taryn would probably kick my butt for letting that slip out. "Not a thing, other than everybody in town thinks Sofia's footed Liam's bills for way too long."

His brows snapped together. "Do you think *Taryn's* paying him? That's not right. I should—"

"Hey." I took his untouched glass and set it on the table along with my own similarly undrunk tea. "I'm not sure of anything, but if you want my opinion? You should just *pretend* that it's true."

"But—"

"Ricky." I held his gaze. "Let it go. Let her do this for Sofia. Let her do it for you."

For a moment, I thought he'd protest, but then he just exhaled slowly and turned back to the window. "That's a hard ask. Tia's so good at taking care of other people. Awesome at it, in fact. But not so great at letting other people take care of her."

"Acts of service," I murmured.

"What?"

"That's her love language. Same as yours."

He gazed at me, an unreadable expression on his face. "Acts of service. Do you think I should… well… pull back a little? Let her take care of me more? Would that make her feel better?"

"Do you think you're capable of that? Stepping back? Because personally, I can't see it."

He sank into a chair, shoulders slumping. "Then what can I do? I hate seeing her like this."

"Maybe the answer is finding somebody other than you for her to focus on." I widened my eyes in mock astonishment, as though something had just occurred to me. "A cousin! Surely there's a cousin somewhere in the Vargas clan who needs some TLC."

He gave me a *seriously?* look. "Vargases are opposed to helplessness on principle. We all know how to get the job done."

"Yes," I drawled. "I'd noticed."

I collected the glasses and ferried them to the sink. As I emptied the tea down the drain, accompanied by the tinkle of unmelted ice, I heard a noise from behind me. I glanced over my shoulder. Ricky was looking down at something in his lap.

"Did you say something?"

"What?" He looked up while shoving his hand into his jacket pocket. His expression was almost... shifty. "No. Nothing."

"Okay." I joined him again and gestured to Sofia. "Do you think she'd like company?"

He shrugged. "Maybe. She's still not saying much, though."

"Then we don't need to talk."

I waited until he rose from the chair and then started for the butler's pantry. I hadn't gone two steps before I froze. I looked down at my hand.

Ricky's fingers were twined with mine.

"Is this all right?"

"Mmmhmmm." I couldn't have made words right if I'd tried.

Because Ricky was holding my hand.

Despite ex damage on both our parts, he'd taken that leap. The least I could do was meet him at that level, and trust that someday our foundation would be sturdy enough to support more.

When we stepped out onto the back porch, I automatically checked behind myself and flinched. *Gil's not here. I don't have to block an escape attempt.*

Ricky must have felt me tense—and correctly identified the reason—because he said, "We'll find him, Maz. Taryn posted it on Ghostline. Everyone in town is looking for him."

"Sure."

So far, nobody had reported so much as a glimpse of him since he'd disappeared. He hadn't pinged Avi's proximity radar even once. I forced a smile and headed down the steps. Ricky let me drop the subject and kept pace with me, our hands still joined, as we walked across the lawn to Sofia.

She smiled at us, but it was clearly a reflex, because she didn't say a word, just returned her gaze to the garden. With a jolt, I realized she was looking at the scarecrow. I glanced sidelong at Ricky. Maybe it was time to ask his cousin to give the scarecrow a makeover.

Ricky squeezed my hand once before letting go to sit on the top step next to Sofia's chair. She rested her palm on his shoulder for a moment, gave it a pat, then clasped her hands in her lap again. I settled on the step below Ricky, close enough that he could press his knee against my shoulder. If, you know, he wanted to do something like that.

Luckily, he did.

The three of us sat there for a moment until suddenly there were four of us. I straightened up, because this was the first time Avi had left the house since that night, even though I always carried Oren's ring with me, just in case.

Avi jerked his head at Sofia and beckoned to me. *Ah. Right.* Ricky knew about him, but Sofia didn't. She might not take it well if I suddenly started talking to what appeared to be empty air.

I stood up and cleared my throat. "Just going to, um, see how the tomato plants are doing." When I joined Avi next to the garden, I made sure to face away from the house so Sofia wouldn't see my lips moving. "What is it? Is something wrong?"

"First, I wanted to apologize."

I glanced at him sidelong. "For what?"

"For invading your privacy." He shoved his hands deep in his cardigan pockets. "I don't have to be visible, you know. When I'm manifesting."

I blinked. "I'd forgotten that. But you were invisible when you stuffed Carson's gun barrel."

"I haven't done it much since then. Until, well, today."

"Oookay."

"I overheard you talking about love languages," he said in a rush, his eyes clenched shut. "I used the Smith Corona and wrote a note for Ricky. I passed it to him just now." He cracked one eye open and peeked at me. "With yours."

I frowned at him. "With my what?"

He faced me fully, his hands on his hips. "Your love language, of course."

"Mine?" I almost threw up my hands until I remembered that checking on tomatoes probably didn't call for such a dramatic gesture. "I don't even know what mine is. Greg certainly complained enough when I didn't offer proper homage to him."

Avi chuckled. "From what you've told me about him, his love language was receiving gifts. Let me guess—when you didn't measure up, he punished you by keeping his distance, right?"

I narrowed my eyes. "How did you know?"

"Because, Maz, your love language is physical touch. Whenever you're upset, the first thing you do is reach for Gil." He waggled a finger at me. "And don't think I haven't noticed the look on your face when you remember you can't pat my shoulder."

"I... have a look?"

"You absolutely have a look. The worst thing Greg could do to you was withhold touch." He jerked his chin at Ricky. "So I thought Ricky should know how you express affection."

I goggled at him. "That's why he took my hand?"

He shrugged one shoulder. "I suspect that was a service he was completely happy to provide. He— Oh!" Avi's eyes widened and his gaze snapped to the bottom of the yard where the seasonal stream burbled among the rocks. "I think... Yes!"

The cattails along the bank rustled and suddenly Gil emerged.

"Gil!" I started to race toward him, but slowed when I noticed he was carrying something in his mouth. "Crap. Is that a rat? Because we didn't have any in the house, he decided to go searching for one?"

"Not a rat, Maz. Look closer."

By that time, Gil was about ten feet away. He uttered a muffled *mrrow* and dropped his burden.

Which moved.

I jumped backward. "Augh!" But then I heard it. A tiny *mew*. "You've got to be kidding me? A *kitten*?"

I crept forward and knelt in the grass. Sure enough, it was a tiny tortoiseshell fluff ball. Not a newborn. Probably at least five or six weeks old because its ears had already migrated to the top of its head and its—*her*, most likely, since most torties were female—eyes had already begun to morph from newborn blue to gold.

I held out my hand, and rather than flinching away from it or hissing, she hopped over and rubbed against my fingers. I scooped her up, and she began to purr immediately. "She's clearly not feral."

"No." Avi ran a finger down her spine, and just like with Gil, her fur reacted to him, lifting in his finger's wake. "The edge of town is a prime dump site for people trying to get rid of unwanted animals. I expect that's what happened to her. It may also be why Gil's been trying so desperately to get out of the house the last couple of days. He probably heard her."

"Good job, buddy." I peered at the kitten's face. Her eyes were clear. She didn't seem to be too undernourished or flea-ridden. "You deserve a—" A burst of panic drove through my middle. "Where did he go?"

Avi jerked a thumb at the ginger tail disappearing into the cattails again. "I don't think he's done."

Sure enough, a moment later, Gil returned with another kitten, this one a black-and-white tuxedo. After he dropped this one at my feet, he sat down and shot out one hind leg, settling in to give himself a bath.

"*Now* I think he's done," Avi said dryly.

"Maz?" Sofia called from the porch, the first time I'd heard her speak since she came home from the hospital. "What do you have there?"

I glared down at Gil. "Don't you dare move." I scooped up the other kitten and turned toward the porch. "Gil found a couple of orphans."

"Oh, pobrecitos. Let me see them." Sofia rose from her chair. Ricky jumped up immediately to help her down the steps. She gave him a look that was almost up to her old standard. "I am not an invalid, Enrique. I can walk across my own lawn."

"Yes, Tia," he said, but stayed by her side as she approached.

"Oh," she breathed. "Bonito. But they must be so hungry." The tuxedo kitten squirmed in my grip and she caught him, cradling him against her cheek to the tune of a purr totally out of proportion to his size. "Will you be keeping them?"

I jerked my thumb at Gil, who'd moved on to his front paws. "Despite his little search and rescue adventure, Gil doesn't like other cats in his territory. Does Ghost have an animal rescue organization?"

"Yes," Ricky said. "It's run by—"

"Let me guess. One of your cousins?"

He just grinned, but Sofia said, "Pfft. We do not need to bother Nayeli about these two. They will have a home here with me." She turned, the tuxedo kitten burrowed against her neck. "Maz, give that little mariposa to Enrique and take your gatito back home. He deserves a treat."

Ricky gently detached the tortie kitten's tiny claws from my T-shirt. "Seems like this one already has a name. Come along,

Mariposa." He paused, then leaned over and kissed my cheek. "Thank you."

"For foisting two kittens on your godmother?"

"No. For being here. For both of us."

"Enrique? Hurry, the pequeños need to eat."

"Coming, Tia."

With Avi still at my side, I hefted Gil in my arms and flipped him upside down as Ricky and Sofia disappeared into the house. After the door closed behind them, I glared down at Gil. "Don't ever scare me like that again."

He did a slow blink, his front paws curled over his furry chest.

"I'm guessing he just said *no promises*," Avi said.

I sighed. "Probably." We headed toward my back porch. "Do you think the kittens will help Sofia recover?"

Avi shoved his hands into the pockets of his chinos. "Help, yes. Completely heal? No."

I snorted as we mounted the steps. "At least she won't need to worry about Liam's alleged allergies for another five to ten years, depending on good behavior. And *that's* just for the aggravated theft charge. Who knows what they'll make of the fraud or the assault charge for swapping out her meds?"

We walked inside and I set Gil on his feet. Predictably, the first thing he did was scamper over to his food dishes and stare at me imperiously.

"Hey, it wasn't *my* idea for you to go on a three-day wilderness hike. What did you eat all that time?" I clapped a hand over my eyes. "No. Don't tell me. I don't want to know."

His kibble dish was full—maybe overfull, because I couldn't keep myself from adding to it every evening, even though he hadn't been there to eat any of it—but I broke out a can of people-tuna. As I was scraping the last bits into his bowl, Avi started to laugh.

I glanced up at him from where I was petting Gil as he chowed down on the chunk white. "What?"

"How long have you been in town, Maz?"

"I don't... Oh, hey. It's one month today."

"And in that month, you've been held at gunpoint, gotten front-ended in the world's shortest car chase, and been instrumental in apprehending two men who've been getting away with—in one case, literal—murder for years. Not incidentally, you're also responsible for the first official beyond-the-veil communication in the town's history, Thaddeus Richdale's obsessive crusade notwithstanding."

"Well, damn. I guess that's true." I stood, not bothering to brush cat fur off my hands, and shook my head. "Whoever claimed small towns were calm and slow-paced had obviously never been to Ghost."

a message from
❧ ej

Dear Reader,

Thank you so much for reading *Ghostlighted*, the second in my Ghost Townies small town cozy mystery series. I'm so happy you've taken this journey with me! I'd be immensely grateful if you'd take a moment to leave a review at the retailer and any other site you use for reviews. Believe me, reviews make an *enormous* difference to the health and well-being of books (and not incidentally, to their associated authors!).

Pop on over to my website, https://ejrussell.com, for all the deets on my books—my paranormal rom-coms and mysteries, my contemporary romances, and my one lone historical. If you're an audio fan, you can find the audio scoop there too. (The QR code on the next page will get you there with your smartphone camera or other code reader.)

Would you like exclusive content and ARC giveaways, not to mention gratuitous dance videos? Then I'd love for you to join me in E.J. Russell's Reality Optional, my Facebook fan group (https://facebook.com/groups/reality.optional). My newsletter is the place to get the latest dish on new releases, sales, and more. I promise I only send one out when I've got…well…news. You can subscribe here: https://ejrussell.com/newsletter.

All my best,
—E

Maz's Dad's Chickpea Salad

Maz's Dad's Chickpea Salad

Serves four to six (unless one of them is Ricky)

Ingredients:

2	15-oz cans chickpeas (garbanzo beans), drained*
1	green bell pepper, cored and diced
6	scallions, chopped
	or
⅓	cup diced onion
1½	cups chopped parsley
¼	cup olive oil (approx.)
1	tsp dried basil
1	tsp dried oregano
	salt and pepper to taste
2	T wine vinegar
2	T lemon juice

Instructions:

1) Combine chickpeas, green pepper, scallions or onion, and parsley; toss with the olive oil.

2) Add basil, oregano, salt, and pepper, tossing after each addition.

3) Add vinegar and lemon juice a little at a time, until desired tartness is reached.

4)　　If salad seems too tart, add a little water or white wine to cut the tartness.

5)　　Chill at least one hour before serving.

*Be sure to get chickpeas that have not had sugar added during the canning process.

Paranormal Romance
Mythmatched Universe
Fae Out of Water Trilogy
Cutie and the Beast
The Druid Next Door
Bad Boy's Bard

Supernatural Selection Trilogy
Single White Incubus
Vampire With Benefits
Demon on the Down-Low

Other Mythmatched Romances
Howling on Hold
Witch Under Wraps
Cursed is the Worst
At Odds with the Gods
The Skinny on Djinni
Assassin by Accident (part of Carnival of Mysteries)

Quest Investigations Mysteries
Five Dead Herrings
The Hound of the Burgervilles
The Lady Under the Lake
Death on Denial

Sign up for E.J.'s newsletter to get the following Mythmatched stories for free!
Possession in Session
Second First Date
Rusty's Really Bad Day
First Flight
Getting the Band Together
Purgatory Postscript
A Very Quest Solstice

Mythmatchedlets (*Second First Date, Rusty's Really Bad Day, First Flight, Getting the Band Together, Purgatory Postscript,* and *A Very Quest Solstice* collected in one paperback volume)

Purgatory Playhouse (part of Magic Emporium

Ghost Townies Mysteries
Ghostridden
Ghostlighted

Enchanted Occasions Series
Best Beast
Nudging Fate
Devouring Flame

Royal Powers Series (shared world)
Duking It Out
Duke the Hall
King's Ex

Supernatural Romantic Suspense
Legend Tripping Series
Stumptown Spirits
Wolf's Clothing

Art Medium Series
The Artist's Touch
Tested in Fire

Science Fiction
Sun, Moon, and Stars
Partnership
Principles

Interdimensional Time Bureau
Monster Till Midnight

Historical Romance
Silent Sin

Contemporary Romance
Camera Shy
Summer Kitchen
The Thomas Flair
Mystic Man
The Probability of Mistletoe
An Everyday Hero
A Swants Soiree
For a Good Time, Call… (A Bluewater Bay novel, with Anne
Tenino)

Geeklandia Series
The Boyfriend Algorithm (M/F)
Clickbait

Writing as Nelle Heran
(traditional cozy mystery)

Crafty Sleuth Series (with C.K. Eastland)

Die Cut
Mixed Media
Found Objects (*coming soon*)

About the
Author

E.J. Russell (she/her), author of the award-winning Mythmatched paranormal romance series, writes LGBTQ+ romance and mystery in a rainbow of flavors. Count on high snark, low angst, and happy endings.

Reality? Eh, not so much.

She's married to Curmudgeonly Husband, a man who cares even less about sports than she does. Luckily, C.H. also loves to cook, or all three of their children (Lovely Daughter and Darling Sons A and B) would have survived on nothing but Cheerios, beef jerky, and Satsuma mandarins (the extent of E.J.'s culinary skill set).

E.J. also writes traditional cozy mystery as Nelle Heran. She lives in rural Oregon, enjoys visits from her wonderful adult children, and indulges in good books, red wine, and the occasional hyperbole.

News & Social Media:
Website: https://ejrussell.com
Newsletter: https://ejrussell.com/newsletter

Acknowledgements

I owe many thanks to my long-suffering editor, Meg DesCamp, not only for keeping my use of *goggled* in check, but for allowing me to include a mention of her humorous gardening book, *Slug Tossing,* here (yes, it's really a thing!). Thanks also to my Darling Son B, Nicholas Katen, for agreeing to be my series cover model; to Sam San Román for photographing him so beautifully; to L.C. Chase for the groovy cover; to lyric apted for beta reading; to NOLAKim, PA extraordinaire, for support (and making sure I'm not a *total* recluse); to the Crit Posse (L.C. Chase, Amy Aislin, and Lee Blair) for cheerleading and reality checks; to my family, who puts up with my eccentricities with only occasional eyerolls.

And, always and forever, thank you to my readers for accompanying me on this journey. You're the reason I can continue to follow my heart, and I appreciate you more than I can say.